I0678536

Battle Planet

Human explorers began to wander back into the forgotten zone. No one knew of the machines that had evolved, or the war that raged beyond the edge of the universe

…where mankind did not belong.

Table of Contents

Titles by Michel Savage

HELLBOT

BATTLE PLANET

MICHEL SAVAGE

Enter the Grey Forest

www.**GreyForest**.com

This is a work of fiction. All the characters, names, businesses, places, and events or incidents portrayed herein are fictitious, and products of the author's imagination. Any resemblance to actual persons, living or dead, or events is purely coincidental.

HELLBOT – Battle Planet

The Grey Forest
P.O. Box 71494
Springfield, OR 97475

www.GreyForest.com

Cover art by Michel Savage

ISBN: 978-0-9719168-9-0

First Edition: March 2010

Printed in the United States of America

0 9 8 7 6 5 4 3 2

Tranquility

Location: Planet; Tranquility
Outpost Station 9

Mission: Water salvage

Log: 141C

Tranquility was one of those out of the way planets in a system far out of reach from the normal space lanes. Loners, dreamers ...whoever they were, chose to colonize this world. Thirty cycles ago something went terribly wrong. It was rumored that their terraformer reactor went critical and few escaped the chain reaction that clouded the atmosphere with a planet-wide sand storm. A decade of hard labor evaporated overnight. What wasn't buried under the ocean of sand was left to fry under the twin suns.

Little is known about the details that devastated the colony, but now water in this sector of the galaxy had become a valued commodity. If there was a chance the settlement's reservoirs were still intact, then their holding tanks could be drained to the last drop, which would be worth twice its weight in credits.

Hell ...it was worth a look.

I made my living as a scavenger, in this trade my kind were commonly considered as nothing more than lower-class outcasts, and were always frowned upon by the general population of humans spread out across the universe. 'Scavy's' they called us, among several other insulting nicknames. We made our living by taking advantage of other people's misfortunes, but as those who suffered such loss were either long dead or missing, there were rarely any contests to salvage claims made on derelict ships or abandoned habitats. Needless to say, out here in the vast plains of space common law was strictly a matter of personal interpretation.

My ship was called the *Valkyrie*, a small cruiser left to me by my estranged father eight cycles ago. His years spent as a part-time scrapyard mechanic and fuel hauler wasn't an easy life in this neck of the cosmos, and it hadn't done much for his personal health either. The official report on record stated he died alone, sometime during a two-week solo shift at a remote mining depot.

It's not like I missed the bastard or anything, I had come to realize that it wasn't his fault that micro-meteors hit the port ring of the orbiting station of Nova 12; nor was he to blame for the structural fractures those impacts caused upon the hull, nor was he responsible for the imminent rupture that resulted in a cataclysmic failure that vented the atmosphere killing my mother and 128 other passengers awaiting transport on layover. The hard facts are that on average, over 30% of all off-world spacers die from a countless array of mishaps that come with the dangers of interstellar travel. It wasn't his fault she became a statistic, but somehow I always felt he should have been there for her …then again, maybe I shouldn't speak ill of the dead.

I got my space-legs working with several crews over the years. Scavy's aren't the most stable bunch of misfits; they come and go with the solar winds. Some get killed on the job while trying to score scrap ships for recycling, or ultimately left bloodied and broken on some barroom floor. Many just get sick of the long hours, rough labor, or insane risks it takes to make a haul worth a credit or two. Pack a half dozen desperate degenerates into a tin can for several months, breathing stale air and forced to smell each others' rancid sweat, and the human species can get mighty hostile with one another over the smallest of things. Out here in the void, you've got to keep your mind busy or you'll lose your sanity.

Despite the risks, I've found I truly preferred going solo. I got used to piloting alone, as long as you've got the right gear and don't bite off more than you can chew, there's nothing wrong with making maximum profit on a haul you don't have to share with several other annoying who only clog up the carbon scrubbers with their stench. I was sole captain of the Valkyrie; fitted with twenty-five triple walled vacuum tanks that I had spent a pretty credit getting vapor cleansed. Sure, my light drive was a little buggy, and the commode didn't work; but she was *my* ship.

I picked up some intel during my last stopover on the 2nd moon of Aries. The first pioneers who discovered that planet found the thick jungles of poisonous plant life that thrived there, filled the atmosphere with an exotic array of extremely toxic gas. It was said that their rotting remains still lie beside their ship down there, entwined within the grasping roots of the native vegetation. Out of convenience, the following survey teams set up a post on one of its orbiting moons, and of course, the first thing they built was a tavern. Surrounded by a tide pool of liquid sulfur, there was an inn where spacers could land for repairs and barter supplies. Nobody remembered the actual name of the moon itself, so they called it by the name of the only bar in town, which was known as 'Pandora's Box'. I've seen many backwards-ass taverns in my time out here in the vacuum, but Pandora had a special charm of its own.

The small moon itself was geologically stable, with vast swamps of silver-tinged sulfur glazing its surface. There were plenty of natural thermal vents that were used to provide electrical power for the outpost, which was its attraction to the first surveyors who landed there. Sometimes, when the thick yellow clouds parted above you could see Aries tinting the sky with its green hue. The only hazard was that outside of your own ship or any enclosed habitat, it was only safe to breathe the air without a respirator for a minute or two, tops.

Aries itself was a lush and attractive world located within the Goldilocks zone, as the scientists put it; just the right distance from its solar star, where it was not too hot, not too cold, but just right. It was one of the rare worlds that were already landscaped with vast amounts of native vegetation; unfortunately, its irony lay in that the plants were exceptionally poisonous to all forms of animal life.

It was a world made entirely of flora with a deadly ecosystem based on toxins. I had a dream once that it was the Garden of Eden, with the roots of the plants feeding off the decaying corpses of Adam and Eve. I was used to having disturbing visions like that but I usually blamed it on my faulty CO_2 scrubbers. Out here in the void, there are no doctors left in the psychiatric field, the last I heard they had all went nuts themselves.

Pandora's Box was a tavern built from the bedrock up,

with a notable combination of both modern design and a touch of nostalgia for ancient Persian architecture. Even though the moon was desolate and barren, the green giant it orbited made up for the lack of color. There was something serene about the yellow mists rising from the silver swamps at sunrise; everything seemed to have a strangely soft yet gentle blur to it, as though you were living in a dream. Like I said before, it had a quaint charm of its own that was hard to forget.

While I was there for the night, I swapped out a few carbon filters and got hit up for a few jobs in the local system. My vessel had originally been a private luxury ship designed for short interplanetary hops until my father upgraded it with a light drive and two dozen tanks after gutting out all the useless fluff. It was all recycled equipment, of course, rescued from the scrap yards, but it worked fairly well. Many who saw my ship wanted to contract the Valkyrie to haul cargo to the next system, but I just had to brush them off with polite excuses, not wanting to reveal that it was outfitted with expensive tanks sealed within the fore and aft of the hull. Exposing that kind of valuable hardware could get one killed out here, or left stranded on some airless rock if you got hijacked.

At least my father taught me one good lesson; don't let anyone take advantage of you and don't back down, ever. "*If someone gives you shit; you feed it back to them in double spoonfuls,*" he would say. But to avoid any hassles, I would just claim I was a lowly deckhand out for a drink while the rest of my temperamental crew of fictional mercenaries were still back onboard the ship. I couldn't let anyone know I was all alone. I heard of many instances where small gangs and port workers alike would conspire to mutiny and pirate a ship right from under the nose of the vessel's captain and crew with hidden weapons they would find a way to smuggle onboard.

I always made sure to wear my thick pulse pistol in full view of any onlookers, so they would know I was well armed and should think twice about screwing with me. I put a few dents and scratches on it intentionally so it would look well-used, and I even wrapped the handle with a strap of real leather I had won on a very costly card bet. I custom tweaked that little bastard so that it had maximum range and would burn a hole through someone, rather than just fry their outer skin. It was useless against steel though, being only made of compressed light, it had to hit something burnable to penetrate before the heat dissipated on impact. New alloy metals that were designed to block all forms of solar radiation were quite common nowadays, and many unsavory scoundrels with ill intent were wise enough to pack plates of it into their vests for use as concealed body armor.

While stretching my legs on Pandora, I was harassed for shipment runs so many times it got to the point where I chose to act like I was just too drunk to be lucid. By chance, that's when I overheard two elderly mine workers from the core system catching up on local rumors. They appeared to be seasoned veterans of the space lanes and had been talking between themselves about an old terraformed world out in the direction of the Omega system. I also keenly noticed they got tight-lipped whenever their barkeep came around, so I just sat slumped with my eyes closed, pretending to be asleep at the table across from them, which also served to help the annoying passer-bys from hassling me. In my line of work I've learned a little snooping into other people's business can be both entertaining and lucrative, either of which is a bonus when you're bored out of your mind.

They talked about a planet I never heard of, they called 'Tranquility', colonized by a few thousand pioneers that went belly up a generation ago. By luck, one of them blurted out the coordinates while he talked in sad tones about an old acquaintance he had lost there. Now, I've certainly heard my fill of bullshit stories in countless taverns around the universe, but this one had a hint of authenticity that raised the hair on the back of my neck. These two old coots seemed to be sincerely afraid of that place. I got goose-bumps when one of them whispered *"...how it was such a waste of all that water,"* that I almost popped my eyes open in shock, which would have revealed I was eavesdropping on them. After a few more drinks, they changed the subject and wandered off. When I was pestered by the server for apparently sleeping at the bar, in full drunken character, I slowly got up and stumbled my way back to the Valkyrie and sealed the hatch.

Planet Tranquility, on the outskirts of the Omega system, why had I never heard of it? Bad news travels fast in space; everyone wants to hear of the disasters that befall other spacers, for their own morbid curiosity. Several thousand colonists getting snuffed in one fell swoop would have made hot news, but apparently, this had happened long before I was even born. Perhaps their story simply got lost among all the drama and other countless tragedies over the past few decades.

Back on board the Valkyrie, I made my way to the database and logged into the local net, letting the computer do the searching on this mystery planet while I checked the star charts. I lounged back in the captain's chair on the bridge while sucking on a partially wrapped food bar; as the swill they were serving back at the tavern was entirely indigestible. My father had installed a responsive computer in the form of an Artificial Intelligence, commonly known as an 'AI' onboard the ship, and he named it '*Valaria*', after my mother. It was a touching thought, but I was glad he hadn't also programmed the ship with her real voice, which would have freaked me out far too much.

"Ala, are you positive the coordinates you entered are correct?" The ship's computer requested, the synthetic voice was gentle enough to be of comfort on these long voyages between jobs; and the outdated AI program was currently my only friend out here in the vacuum.

"Yes, Val, what have you got?" I mumbled between bites of the bland nutrition bar, which had been the major staple of my diet these past few years, as it was for most poor spacers like me who couldn't afford to stock decent food.

"Chart authentication for the requested target has failed on all three versions of the universal navigational database," the AI answered.

"Well," I wandered off with a thought, "…try sifting through any common charts on record that's older than 30 years, and let me know what you get," I suggested.

"Searching…" Val trailed off as a few of the lights blinked whenever the computer was drawing more than its fair share of power, "There are no charts on record in range of two million parsecs of the Omega system within those specified parameters, Ala."

That admission made me frown. I really didn't like

being stumped with mysteries; I just wanted to know all the facts upfront. Star charts were never deleted, no matter how old they were. The galaxy was vast and all information ever compiled was stored and updated on Earthnet; which was the universal charting service available for all ships and unmanned probes. Some suggested that the military had their own secret charts, but the arm of the law didn't reach this far out into the void. Then again, maybe this was just a frivolous waste of time and those drunken old farts had blabbered out the wrong coordinates by mistake, or there was something fishy going on if an entire system had been deliberately deleted from the public database. That's when I remembered something key that almost slipped by me in their conversation.

"How many twin star systems are there in that area?" I asked, remembering one of the old-timers had mentioned something about a double sunrise.

"More than half of *all* solar systems are binary, Ala, do you still wish me to compute that number?" The ship answered.

I choked on my last bite of the meal bar; more than half are twin stars? I almost didn't believe her, but the computer never lies, it just spits out hard facts. I've been to a few systems that had been comprised of twin or triple stars, but until now, I had thought they were only rare exceptions.

"Never mind, Val," I shrugged, almost giving up on the whole scheme, but then again, maybe there was some bits of history on that place left floating around after all these years. "…on second thought, do a data search for anything like a planet or colony named Tranquility between the past 25 to 35 cycles from this Stardate, then optimize the results with any records of missing civilians with a headcount over 1000, and let me know what you come up with."

"Time estimate is 8.4 hours to compile those results, Ala," the computer informed. Not exactly being known for my patience, I sighed loudly and conceded to initiate the request. During that time there would be a limited power drain while the computer fed on the core, so no sonic shower to wash off this lingering stench of sulfur while it was working on the data, so I might as well take a nap in my bunk. Shuffling back to my quarters, I had taken over the entire upper deck of the crew's chambers for my own. Since I had gone solo, it was only a matter of an imaginative use of power tools to break down a cramped cabin of six bunks and convert it into something more livable.

Honestly, I had always been tempted to disassemble the Freezer for some extra room, which are what we spacers called the cryogenic units we used for extended light drive runs. There's nothing like shoving yourself like a meat sack into a cramped cabinet to be frozen for the first time. A gas tube attached to your nose turns your blood to gel so you can defrost after several weeks or months without having to waste food, air, or stop up the waste disposal full of crap. I really hated using them; those fucking things always left me with an unshakable migraine for several hours and a queer stench like rancid lemons lingering in my skull; then again, I owned one of the outdated bargain basement models. Every time I picked up a wrench to break it down, I cowered out. Despite the side effects, freezers did help curb the number of spacers who went loony from spending too much time in the void.

Anyone who tells you that they don't have lucid dreams while playing Popsicle in one of those stasis tubes, is bullshitting you; everyone seems to come out a little different, as if they left a piece of themselves behind in la-la land. The strange thing is, when you wake up, even colors seem to be a little off; certain scents bring back memories of graphic dreams or nightmares of places that never existed. It was a real trip if you approached it with the right mentality; and they were better than any drug. From time to time, you hear rumors of spacers who get addicted to it and put themselves under for no reason, or for insanely long stretches. The human species wasn't meant to screw with their bodies and metabolism as much as we have.

Artificial intelligence programs installed in ships not only help with navigation but keep people from making stupid mistakes and causing fatal accidents; little things, like forgetting to pressure lock a hatch before launch can ruin your day, although with a little effort you can bypass any safety protocol. There was a time decades ago when it was a fad to own a companion droid for shits n' giggles. They were actually quite useless, and took up a great deal of unnecessary weight when you thought about it. Most bots were actually used for automated transport or as labor in harsh environments, including mass fabrication on construction projects for habitats and orbital stations.

I've seen holographic pictures of terraformer colonies using truly massive robots to erect buildings and greenhouse domes, boring wells, or laying pipe, you name it. They were the altered remnants from power-suits and robotic crawlers used during the resource wars several generations ago. Mankind has been exploring space for several centuries now, but there was the time when our numbers were drastically thinned. Earth had been turned into a real shit-hole, with its dirty oceans and stagnant air, nobody wanted to live there. I think the historical records said more people were living in orbiting stations than in the ruined cities spread across the globe back then.

From what I read, it was a really crappy time to be alive and Earth-bound; although, when light drive technology came along it changed everything. It works by direct line of sight between any two star systems, the light drive wraps around the concentrated beam of light and climbs the spectrum of electromagnetic wavelengths; continually cycling upon itself at ever-increasing speeds, thereby 'pulling' the craft to the distant star well beyond light speed. Supposedly, the spectrum is infinite and continuous, though honestly, I never understood all the mathematics of it. Apparently, it was the best god-damn thing mankind ever created; so now our species can spread across the universe like locusts and crap on other pristine worlds.

I don't mean to be so negative, but after growing up in salvage yards and recycling other people's refuse my entire life as I have, you don't exactly end up having a great appreciation for the human race. Human beings can be downright ugly and selfish, that's reason enough as to why I ended up going solo. It seems some people are only satisfied with their lives when they can beat others down or taunt them with their own unbalanced psychosis. Personally, I can't put up with that kind of stress without being tempted to blast a hole through someone. Just then, the AI came back online with a jolt.

"Analysis complete, Ala, would you like to hear the

results now?" Valaria requested.

What the fuck… had I been laying here awake with my mind racing all this time?

"So soon?" I blurted in disbelief.

"It's been 8.5 hours since you initiated the search request," Val's voice answered. Holy shit, neurosis confirmed! I must really be going nuts after all.

"Sure, shoot," I shrugged as I sat up in my bunk.

"There were 8,014 references to the name 'Tranquility' associated with colonies; 64 were names of moons and minor planetoids, however, nearly all of those were located in the Regal Galaxy at the opposite end of the universe," Valaria concluded, "The majority were names of settlements, hauling, and transport ships or mining outposts," the computer added.

"And you filtered out the ones with twin suns?" I yawned, feeling mentally weary.

"Yes Ala, there were only two minor references within that 10-year timeframe with civilian casualties of one thousand or more," she answered as the data popped up on the video screen, so I got up and waddled over to get a closer look.

Framed on the display was an old advertisement for a terraforming project called *Avalon* that was hiring workers and pioneer families on a 15-year contract. It was one of those ludicrous ads that showed laughing children playing with toy rockets, while their parents poised in immaculate clean clothes with glazed eyes and wide smiles stretched across their faces. Blue skies and lush greenhouses towered in the background with other indiscernible figures milling about, as if it were all some grand example of civilization in progress. Across the top were bold letters **'Build it your way!'** What a goddamn sick joke.

Ridiculous ads like this were used to lure in desperate suckers who would only come out of transport stasis to find themselves trapped upon some inhospitable planet in far worse condition than they were informed it would be when they had initially signed on, and not knowing they had just condemned themselves and their families to inescapable hardship for the next decade or more, as terraforming planetary atmospheres didn't produce livable results until the process was nearly 90% complete. Even then, it was an endless cycle of ozone and moisture farming to keep the greenhouses alive. In most cases, the climate was so unforgiving that even pioneers who were given land as part of the bargain would give up everything they'd worked for and skip planet the very hour their contracts came full term.

The sponsoring corporations didn't care; as they maintained mineral rights and got a free starbase built out of the process, and would simply reclaim any abandoned plots for additional profit. In reality, it actually took well over sixty years or more to transform a planet to even be worth looking at, and the average lifespan of a spacer was only around forty ...in any sense, it just didn't equate. The first ad was addressed by several dead links and missing news references, though it stated their flag colony would support 8,000 plus in the fine print below. Besides, greenhouses meant water, and lots of it. I had seen such project habitats before, and the enormous silos they used for storage.

The 2nd search result was a simple text record of a corporate loss denied in some confusing jargon by its insurance agency. One might expect these kinds of records were usually kept confidential, but there was a news link to a mass exodus from the Avalon project for reasons that were unclear. There were additional sub-paragraphs mentioning a paid settlement of the monetary kind, but several lines and footnotes in the data had been clearly deleted. Well, it was better proof than none. This far out in the void, water was leeched and recycled from bodily fluids to sewage, which was truly disgusting when you thought about it. I heard tall tales that on old Earth, spring water was so fresh and clear it was both odorless and tasteless. Living in artificial environments most of your life, spacers got used to the tinge of metal and plastic in their water supply. Farming water from gas planets or asteroids was so horrifically expensive it wasn't worth the effort. Let alone the resources needed to start projects of that magnitude. At one time on Earth, there used to be vast tundra's of pure ice the size of continents at its poles, I shit you not! But of course that all melted away into the polluted oceans as did every glacier on the planet more than a century ago. What a miserable waste.

Even so, it would be too expensive to transport liquid H_2O between the stars. You had to find it locally or it wasn't worth the trouble. The gas planet Aries, which Pandora orbited was a good example, as there was a water-like substance that was far more than abundant in its atmosphere; but alas, like many other alien worlds, its chemical make-up had extra molecules attached, making it caustic, besides the fact that the water vapor there was saturated with exotic toxins, and its strange molecular binding made it impossible to filter out. Thus were the joys of space travel, colonists searching the galaxy for another Earth-like Eden, because we had abused and ass raped our own homeworld like a 5-credit whore.

Hypothetically, mankind could have survived nicely on Earth if it had balanced around a five to six hundred million people, but once the population tipped over 20 billion, we were completely fucked. So we spread out across the galaxy to get some shoulder room and ended up shanking each other for overstressed resources from the home-world and abroad. Mankind, being its own worst enemy, whittled itself down to less than 6 billion in the resulting civil and interstellar wars that followed. Pirates and mercenaries ruled the seas of space back then, and a lot of heroic tales of grandeur live on from that violent time; though we nearly killed off every beneficial species of animal and insect on our planet from the resulting pursuit of bloodshed and destruction.

After a long moment of hard thought and a tally of my credits, I thought I would give this a gamble. Though the evidence that this planet even existed was notably scarce and entirely absent from the published star charts, made it even more enticing for a treasure hunting scavenger like myself; so I followed my gut feeling.

"Val, prep the Freezer and compute a flight plan to the coordinates I gave you on Tranquility," I requested.

"Are you sure, Ala?" The ships AI asked gently, "My current data shows no recorded system in that sector."

"No …I'm not really all that sure, actually," I hesitated, "but we'll find out the hard way."

Outpost 9

Ala awoke from stasis with the horrid stench of rotting citrus left floating in her head. There were a few hypos left in the medical cabinet that would help dull the hangover but they were god-awful expensive; so she figured she would wince this one off. It was impossible to get back to sleep after being defrosted; the process required that you had to stay up and moving to keep blood pumping to your extremities for the next hour, regardless, lest there was the risk that the residual freezer burn would liquefy your veins.

"Good morning Ala," the ship's AI stated gently. The computer always offered warmly whenever she came out of cryo-sleep, despite the fact there was no day or night while in space, but she had never bothered to change the program. Even though her head was pounding at the moment, Ala's curiosity got the best of her.

"So, did we jump out into the middle of nowhere, Val?" The girl responded with a cynical tone.

"Actually, there are two targets within range; one is a binary system with similarities to your initial search directive. The second, is a young star in its early stage of development," Valaria confirmed.

"Are there any habitable planets?" Ala inquired while rubbing her eyes in a vain effort to suppress her throbbing headache.

"The binary star has eight planetoids, two of which are drastically off the central orbital plane in relation to the gravitational ellipse and would not be able to support life," the AI responded, "four are gas planets, and two more are without any primary atmosphere and have an exceptionally erratic rotation. There is only one other that has evidence of previous colonization."

Even though the young pilot had a migraine pounding at her skull, she could still count.

"But that would make nine planets, you said there were eight?" Ala responded questionably. When the computer started making mistakes that was the time to worry. Hell, she hadn't run a systems diagnostic for as long as she could remember.

"In technical terms, Ala, there are eight planets. The habitation is located on a moon of one of the gaseous solar bodies, specifically the one with the predominant ring," Valaria countered in defense.

"Are we in orbit around it now?" Ala jumped up to put some clothes back on and hustled towards the bridge so she could see what the the computer was talking about.

"No Ala, we are still 5 parsecs from the binary system," the AI advised. 'What happened?' She thought to herself, 'did we drift out of light drive between the two systems?' Five parsecs was a whole lot of empty space to cover.

"Can you correct our heading and jump us closer Val?" Which was more of a demand than a request; it was aggravating when the navigational array went screwy.

"That would be inadvisable," the computer responded.

"And why is that?" Was all she asked, though Ala felt like seriously cussing her out. 'Now where the fuck did I put that maintenance manual for doing systems diagnostics?' Ala whined to herself while she got up and made a half-assed attempt to look around the cabin as the ship answered.

"The two elliptical planets I had mentioned before, cross our line of sight. I still have not computed their trajectories across our flight plan," she answered to the girl's aggravation.

"What the hell, they're goddamn planets for Christ's sake, Val, you would think we would see them coming! Just head us in towards that moon," Ala ordered with impatience. Freezer headaches always left her in a foul mood, and didn't do much for her manners either.

"Actually, Ala, their elliptical orbits are exceptionally unstable as both planets are pulling on one another..."

"So fine, I think you would notice *two* planets barreling at us and evade their orbital path. Is there something wrong with your navigational array you're not telling me about, Val? Crap! ...I knew I should have done an overhaul on that bloody wiring two months ago on Regis-5," she blurted out loud to herself.

"The ship's navigational array is working properly Ala," the AI confirmed, "The problem is not from the two orbiting solar bodies per se, but the amount of debris following in their wake."

"Huh?" Ala finally got her pants on and boots buckled with a free arm to grab her overcoat to fight the nip in the air, because she had been too cheap to buy a timer circuit for the heating coils embedded in the air ducts.

"Due to their proximity and gravitational stresses, combined with the speeds involved, the back half of each of the two elliptical planets has been shattered and they are followed by a shower of their own debris," the ship stated to the girl's alarm.

"*Annnd*, just how big of a debris field are you talking about, Val?" Ala inquired with a sinking-feeling in her gut, that knowing her luck, they had drifted right into the oncoming path of the mother of all meteor storms.

"Incalculable. It would take approximately 3 hours to

discern the trajectories with the ships limited resources and only 29% of those results could be considered reliable for necessary course corrections or evasive maneuvers. Though inadvisable at this time, would you like me to start compiling the calculations for you, Ala?" The computer had the audacity to ask her as she tromped up the galley to the bridge where her captain's chair sat with a light film of frost still layered upon it.

"And it's inadvisable at this time because…?" She led on, being used to prying the logistics out of the simple-minded computer.

"Because the two solar entities mentioned are due to cross our position within the next hour," the AI replied.

"*Within* the next hour? Could you be a bit more specific?" She asked again with a raised brow while punching up the data on the console. Outside the bridge window, Ala could see the distant young star Valaria had mentioned, and she had to pump the thrusters to turn the ship in towards the binary system. The ship rocked while the starfield out front rolled sideways as the boosters corrected their attitude. The bright light of the twin suns, locked in perpetual orbit, suddenly glazed through the cockpit window as the ship turned about. The young pilot immediately spotted a gas giant adorned with its wide ring of ice particles and asteroids. Ala had the navigation array lock a visual on the moon as the computer responded to her inquiry.

"Yes, within, as in under the next hour; and, no, I cannot be more accurate without going offline to compute the current data," the ship replied.

"But we're so far out from the core system it'll take nearly three days on pulse drive alone just to reach it," Ala whined.

"Four days, five hours, using the main drive; as this system has not been charted, it is inadvisable to commit a jump," the computer cautioned, and Ala knew it was a fair warning at that. There were a number of hazards from black asteroid fields to invisible radiation belts that could end your trip on a bad note if you jumped blind. At those speeds there is no such thing as evasion, you and your ship both get annihilated and become a permanent part of the stellar landscape. Every spacer has nightmares about that kind of thing; anyone who tells you otherwise, is lying.

"Well, how far do we have to go to get clear?"

"The calculations are incomplete, and as mentioned, even current data is less than 30% reliable, or more accurately, 71.4% flawed," Valaria advised.

Ala couldn't blame the computer for taking the ship out of light drive and leaving them like sitting ducks in the middle of an oncoming meteor storm, after all, she was the one who had punched in the jump coordinates herself. Interactive navigational computers were great for following instructions, but not known for exercising a great deal of common sense. Well, she had better come to a decision fast or the Valkyrie would end up as a million pieces of pulverized scrap metal.

"Can you take us out of harm's way, Val?"

"Please note, Ala, without the proper data, there is a 2/3rds chance we will move further into the path of the approaching event," she stated flatly.

"Well shit! At least get us moving instead of just sitting here with your thumb up your ass," Ala yelled, angry at herself for getting into this situation like an idiot. Her burning headache wasn't helping either. If she was going to get slammed into a planet or ripped to shreds in the hail of rock to follow, she might as well use those last few hypos; so Ala stomped back to the cabinet and used the only two she had left. After a moment, she was finally thinking straight again.

"Val, if we're this far out of the system, how the hell could you tell there was a colony moon down there?"

"Because there is a navigation buoy in orbit around it," she admitted finally, "which is broadcasting a warning."

"Huh, what kind of a warning?" The girl asked with slight hesitation. With the gears in her head spinning, the pieces were falling into place. Considering the circumstances, it was very likely that this moon was the elusive settlement of Tranquility after all.

"Not to land," was all the ship said.

"That's it?" The girl replied with a shrug of confusion.

"That is all," the AI confirmed, "which appears to be looped on a repeating cycle on all frequencies."

That got Ala thinking; perhaps the colony ran into some serious problems and had to abandon the project, then placed a warning buoy as they departed out of regard for other pioneers, or possibly as a clever ruse to keep salvagers away. But then, if someone was trying to hide this place, a buoy would only serve to attract attention; it didn't make any sense. After tapping into the signal from the orbiting satellite, it confirmed what Valaria had said. Then Ala noticed that there was a line of data in the sub-frequency, all generic information about the satellite moon itself. She had the computer give her the specs on record. Glancing out the port window, she noticed something odd; a section of space where the stars were being blotted out one by one.

Turning the scope in the general direction of the anomaly, the sensors began to scream. Like a solid impassible wall, the incoming reflection took up the entire radar screen.

"The two solar bodies are on a collision course with us. Ala, what are your instructions?" The ship asked calmly.

After quickly scanning the board, it was clear there was no way in hell they could outrun nor maneuver around this tsunami of rock coming at them like a tide of death. Another alternative was just to reverse course and jump back to Pandora, which would have been an option had she committed to it the moment she came out of hyper-sleep; unfortunately the arc of the two dead planets had just blotted out the vital line-of-sight needed for light drive to function. They were fucked!

"Val, check that buoy for any rudimentary data, and use the carrier wave to upload it to our navigational banks." It only took a few tense minutes for the computer to stream the information onto the screen.

Each second that passed, several more stars in the distance blinked out. Something that large can seem very deceiving as to how fast it's actually moving. Her guess was she had less than 20 minutes before they got slammed with the percussion wave at its forefront. That kind of anomaly doesn't exactly show up on a scanner but was something she had learned from experience during her years as a spacer. The buoy data was old, but she found what she had hoped would be there; navigational data about their orbiting planets. One of the first things a corporate scouting team would do is to perform a complete reconnaissance mapping of the solar system they wanted to populate. Hopefully, it was something she could use.

"Good work, Ala, I can compute a flight plan from the attached data," the AI commented with a favorable tone.

"Well, make it snappy," Ala responded with a worried glance at the scanner screen. Light drive engines took a while to activate, and she had to turn the ship directly towards the nearest of the two stars. It wasn't meant to be used this way; jumps were usually made from system to system between two solar bodies. Since they were doing a dead jump, the calculation had to be accurate or they would either wind up way too close on an uncontrolled entry into the atmosphere, or bypass their target altogether and wind up submerged in the sun's corona; either way, that meant they would likely be fried.

"Flight plan complete, shall I initiate our jump, Ala?"

"This is not the time for stupid questions, Val!" She blurted back at the computer.

In the forefront of the wave, particles of asteroids had just begun pelting the hull at an increasing rate. The shields activated and the countdown began. Ala knew Valaria only asked such an obvious question because going into light drive while out of cryo-stasis could cause a number of health hazards, but being pancaked between two erratic planets was at the top of her list of concerns …three, two, one, initiate.

Without the proper shielding, they say you can go blind jumping like this out of stasis; something about the gel of the inner eye losing cohesion. Then again, there are also a lot of rumors about other more colorful abuses to the human anatomy that can make you go blind. However, Ala personally enjoyed it; when you jump out of stasis, there's a kind of strange euphoria that ripples down your body, making your entire being feel like a sensual organ for a millisecond or two. It's the afterglow she liked best; you just sit there shivering over the lingering sensation. She could understand how some spacers became addicted, for those few that had experimented with it. Of course, the lack of shielding, which a stasis tube provides, substantially exaggerates the effects, including upping the chance of causing a number of undesirable and debilitating side effects.

They had dangerously overshot their stop point; the Valkyrie came out of light drive and began to drift into the gravitational pull of one of the inner planets; a pale violet gas giant with rolling clouds of sulfuric oxide. Fine ice particles pelted the hull as the orbital boosters cut in. It always took a few moments for the computer to reboot since jumps sucked 100% of the juice from the power core. It would cost far more than Ala had seen in a lifetime to refit this ship with modern upgrades. She was just a poor scavy after all; if this job went well, then she might be able to change all that.

"Correcting attitude," Valaria cut in as she pulled their ship out of the gravity well, "that was close, Ala, had the drive taken another nanosecond we…"

"…We would have been vaporized," Ala finished for her as she gazed back at the furious spinning planet outside the window; mad storms swirling through its ionosphere hiding a hostile landscape that could have very well been her grave. It was a ripe example as to why you should never dead-jump blind without properly updated navigational data.

"I don't need to remind you that was reckless, Ala, but considering the alternatives available at the moment, it was an acceptable risk," the computer noted.

"Don't chastise me, Val; we're still in one piece, and that's all that matters."

Over the past several years she had put herself, this ship, and its crew in several tight spots. But by its nature, life as a spacer was a gamble; always has been, always will be. In comparison, Ala had always considered the life of a settler was far too timid for her taste; limited to eking out a living on some forgotten rock was a form of surrender in her opinion. This ship had become her home, and it was all she had left of her family. Ala wasn't as emotionally strong as she led others to believe, but her losses and experiences had tempered her in a way different from most people who milled about in their boring lives planet-side. That analogy would apply to most spacers who felt at home, even while lost among this vast ocean of stars.

Valaria put them on a heading towards the lunar body. The warning buoy verified that this was in fact Tranquility, the lost colony of the long-forgotten settlement project sponsored by a mega-industrial business entity called the REVO Corporation. It took some digging through the uploaded files to confirm this was the location of the flag colony for the Avalon project. Tranquility wasn't all that attractive from space; there were vast deserts and patches of gray, and a considerable number of mountain ranges. Of significant note were great canyons and that usually meant a water table once ran topside. Subsurface pockets of moisture could be drilled and pumped up to the surface. It was mostly confusing, as she never understood all the engineering crap involved with full radius planetary terraforming and environment altering technology applied on such a global scale.

She took a few extra minutes to visually scan the chart, but she couldn't find any large signs of vegetation. Such abandoned greenhouses would frequently run rampant on their own, however, those instances were very rare.

This planet seemed hard up for moisture, though there were apparent storm fronts that had collected in the thick atmosphere. Ala had a few hours to burn as they made their way closer to the planet, so she reviewed some additional data the buoy held. To her surprise, there was a generic chart embedded in the data banks, so she chose one at random. Outpost 9 of section four on grid twelve, seemed as good as any other to target in on. The bandwidths were clear, and there was no radio traffic except for the ping from the orbiting buoy.

She had spent nearly half of her plasma core just to get out to this forsaken wasteland, and had to find something of value or else she would be hard up for credits to buy fuel when she got back. A quarter-million gallons of water would let her live in luxury for a long while; the young pilot could only hope that the settlement's silo tanks had not cracked and bled into the soil. Ala prayed that she was the first spacer out this way since the planet was abandoned. From the rumors she had overheard back on Pandora, no one had bothered to come back ...they said the place was cursed.

"Take her in, Val, and let me know if you pick up any movement or activity on the broadband. I don't want to get jacked by pirates out here," she stated firmly as the AI confirmed the instructions.

Desperate spacers would do anything to make a score since there was no real form of law enforcement out here in the void; and certainly not this far from the space lanes. Ala strapped in for the approach as she recorded a log entry during their descent. The engines left a wake of hot plasma during the flyby of Outpost 9. There were several such water stations on the planet, but the majority of them were now buried under a vast sea of shifting dunes.

The ship started its landing sequence while Ala took a look out the starboard window. Distant sandstorms left a haze in the air; she didn't want to stay here too long as this fine grit would clog every crevasse of the ship. Her vessel was already equipped with several hundred meters of tubing that she could use to pump the water reservoir dry and deposit its contents into her holding tanks, but first, she had to find out if their underground silos were still intact.

As the Valkyrie came into the landing approach, the distant gas giant began to rise over the horizon. Ala had seen skylines of many alien worlds, but this one seemed somehow ...unsettling. The gravity thrusters kicked in, blowing up a plumage of dust and sand, and the ship set down gently onto the hot surface several dozen yards from the station. There was an exceptional amount of sand piled up around the building and its main entry, but nothing she would need a shovel for.

"O^2 levels are barely within acceptable range, and the air quality is poor. I would suggest you don't exert yourself too much, Ala," the ship's computer advised as the girl made her way to the lower deck. The atmosphere panel lit green and a sudden suction of pressure popped her ears as the whirring motors opened the exterior hatch and lowered the ramp. Some say certain scents can trigger memories, and Ala would never forget the first time she smelled the dusty wind of this desolate moon. It reminded her of something oddly familiar, a moment from her childhood, but she couldn't quite grasp the vision of what it was.

Ghosts

Ala stepped out onto the hot sand and made her way towards the station as dust caked upon her boots. It appeared the entire structure was half-decayed by a type of alien rust, having turned the exterior of the building a dark brown. Luckily, the entry portal was unlocked but ended up being a real bitch to pry loose. As the door creaked open she wasn't too surprised to find the interior also layered with sand, having found its way in through minute crevices in the bunker over the long years. Considering the seals must have failed long ago, it felt just as hot in here as the arid landscape outside. Some people get spooked entering abandoned buildings, which anyone would guess is a natural human reaction to something strange and unfamiliar; but by the nature of the job it was something that you became accustomed to after a time.

Superstitious scavengers simply don't get very far in this line of work. Ala had scouted dozens of shipwrecks and deserted colonies, and you learn not to jump at every knock or rattle you hear, you have to learn to trust your eyes. Your ears alone can conjure up all sorts of imaginary specters, which can make you lose your nerves or cause a distraction that might easily end up getting you killed. Turning the corner down the hall, however, Ala was still shocked to find a corpse, the decimated remains of some female technician who had been caught here during the catastrophe. The body was huddled in the corner of the control room, her skin darkened; the crust of her flesh preserved by the dry desert heat.

Ala had seen her share of cadavers, some in better shape than others. It wasn't clear what had killed the woman, as there were no obvious wounds. To a scavy, the presence of dead bodies was seen as a good sign, as there were likely no salvage claims to the property at hand. Clearly, the REVO Corp had never returned to clean up their mess after all these years. That lifted her spirits, as it meant this place was ripe for looting. It would be a hell of a lot of work for one person, but the profits would be worth the effort.

The body lay huddled in the corner under a console next to a long window caked over with dirt. The gray keyboard of the control panel had an uncommon configuration, but not terribly difficult to decipher. Ala hit the dial on the console and the frame slowly blinked to life; luckily the solar panels lining the roof were still operational. She nervously accessed the memory system for data on the station while sparing a glance to the carcass lying by her feet.

The display lit up with flashing icons as it brought up a layout of the drilling station and began to run a diagnostic status on the level of the reservoirs. For some reason, no information relayed on the chart; she would have to inspect them manually. Ala brought up the grid chart on the station and turned to make her way out of the control room to the section where the storage tanks were indicated to be installed. Far out of character for her; Ala jumped when she heard a faint whisper behind her, and pulled her blaster from its worn holster in a flash. Looking around, there was nothing. Ala took another troubled glance over at the silent corpse; for some reason this place was getting to her nerves, which could lead to making a careless mistake since she was on her own.

"Get a grip Ala, there's no such thing as ghosts," she muttered to herself.

The chart had shown the moisture tanks were buried underground, three levels below. Down the hall, Ala passed another open doorway that led to stairs up to the access towers and observation decks. However, the hallways below ground level were wide and sloped as they descended to the lower floors, apparently to allow for carting large equipment. As she took the slanting passage down to the lower decks, Ala noticed something very peculiar up ahead that hadn't been marked on the diagram. There was a paneled corridor here which led to a tunnel bored into the rough bedrock itself, which seemed strangely out of place.

At the bottom, she was staring into the darkness of the third level chamber at the end of the hall where the silos should have been. Where were the moisture tanks? Her curiosity nagged at her where the containers had disappeared to; but then, she didn't have much of a choice in the matter, she had to find water somewhere on this damned moon or she would be hard up for funds by the time she made it back. Ala had gambled too much coming this far out into the void all alone.

The lights in the hallway flickered in defiance from their decades of stasis as she stomped back up the ramp to the mysterious panel covering the entrance to the rocky corridor. Cupping her hand over the glass to cut out the reflection of the hallway lights, her touch activated the sensor, which raised the pane into the ceiling above. Unlike the brown sandstone on the surface, the rock strata present here was strangely colored in a mix of turquoise hues. She felt the smooth texture of the stone as she made her way into the darkness; it was strangely rippled, like some sort of marbleized membrane.

Slowly making her way through the dark tunnel, her senses perked as she felt the sudden coolness of a breeze and the humidity which it carried. There was water here! She stumbled into a vast underground cavern containing a deep clear pool, the sound of her boots echoed against the distant walls mixing with the drops of water that resounded in chorus. A wide smile crossed her face, even though she was more than slightly puzzled why this cache was not being held in a sterile tank as shown on the diagram charts. Measuring it out in her head, it was possible that the Valkyrie had enough tubing to reach down this far to pump most of it out. She was sure whatever native contaminants it might contain could be handled by the ion filters aboard the ship. Yes, this would do nicely; there was enough water here to fill more than half of the onboard tanks, and if she was lucky, all she had to do was find one more station to top it off and she could get off this lousy rock.

Ala turned to make her way back to retrieve the tubing when something unusual caught her eye; a faint glow from within the pool itself growing brighter by the second. Standing transfixed in wonder, a ball of blazing light rose to the surface. Ala stumbled backward, shielding her eyes. Electrical arcs shot out from the flaming orb as a bright ghostly figure appeared in its place. She could swear that the apparition faintly resembled the deceased female technician lying in the control room.

Out of instinct, she moved to draw her gun when there

was a sudden blinding, flash and everything went black. Images of faded colors and translucent bubbles filled her head like the cryogen-induced nightmares that you can't awaken from. Flashes of strange plants in even stranger colors, passing so quickly that she couldn't describe them; then quite suddenly there was nothing but a dark dead silence.

Ala felt cold stone beneath her as she stirred. She didn't know how long she had lain there unconscious, but noticed her hair and skin were now soaking wet … had she fallen into the subterranean pool? Ala choked and coughed up water uncontrollably to clear her lungs. Her whole body ached in a way she had never felt before, down to her very bones. Looking at her wet hands, it took a few moments for her brain to realize that her gloves and her coat; in fact, all of her clothes were now missing. She stood there naked, stumbling to her feet while barely catching herself from falling into a deep void. Ala was no longer in the shallow cave, but on a high ledge within a large cavernous chamber.

Between where she stood and the opposite wall spanned a bridge of stone balanced precariously across the dark chasm below; in its center stood a cylinder of light, glowing with a life of its own. Though aching and dazed as she felt, Ala realized no human colonist had built this place. She put her hands at her side, absently noticing, once again, that both her belt and weapon were also gone.

Disoriented and confused, she cautiously turned to inspect her surroundings; she was surprised to find that set within the wall behind her stood a portal of rippling water, a vertical doorway of liquid held back by something she could not understand. With a glance towards the dark emptiness above her and below, rather than entering the wall of water and risk drowning, she chose to make her way across the unearthly bridge. Narrow steps led up to a pedestal of light, upon which sat a small sphere, solid yet strangely alluring; small enough to hold in the palm of her hand. The glowing mist surrounding it held it aloft somehow. The affliction of Ala's innate curiosity won over caution as she slowly reached for this shining gem, only to have it erupt in a flash of light. For a second time, everything in her conscious went dead black.

There were no images or strangely colored dreams to swim through her head this time; the only experience she could recall was that of complete and suffocating darkness filled with nothing but a drumming silence…

*   *   *

When she awoke, the first thing she could perceive was the wind howling in her ears as bits of warm sand were pelting her exposed skin. It took a moment for her eyes to adjust to the brightness as a pair of suns burned the scorched dunes around her. As she struggled to prop herself up, Ala felt that odd ache again, accompanied by a lingering feeling of calmness; the kind you experience when you fly high above the clouds where no living creature has ever been, and can't help but be captured by the serene beauty of someplace you don't belong.

Ala's lips were dry as was every inch of her exposed skin. There was only the bright sunlight and howling wind flooding into her ears, and the faint clanking of metal. It took all of her energy just to sit up, only to notice her clothes were still gone. Ala had been hoping the memory of what she had seen left swimming in her mind was just the remnants of a bad dream. As she gazed out over the dunes with her blurry eyes, it was apparent she was still on Tranquility, but where?

A bit dazed, she glanced around without being able to begin to contemplate exactly what had happened to her. She found herself sitting in the shadow of a half-buried transport of some sort; a broken-down cargo shuttle perhaps, it was hard to tell as she didn't recognize anything of its design. A loose piece of metal on its side was flapping in the desert breeze. Standing up, she took a few steps up the dune that had formed around the wreckage and looked out over the barren landscape. Neither the Valkyrie nor the high tower of Outpost 9 was anywhere in sight. Somehow she had been stripped of everything and left abandoned somewhere upon this unforgiving stretch of desert. Ala's head began to clear as the haze of a distant sandstorm came creeping over the horizon, and she started to become worried as the full realization of her predicament began to sink in.

This was supposed to have been a hit and run mission, so she had never bothered to review the planetary cycle of this moon. As one sun set, the other was soon to follow and Ala could certainly tell the change in temperature almost immediately. Huddling next to the buried wreckage to protect herself from the biting wind, the girl took a moment for a closer inspection to see what she could use to make a shelter. The thick metal shell of the machine wasn't going to give, but she did find a bar with a hooked end and ground it with a stone to give it a sharp edge along its tip.

She was hoping this planet was devoid of any dangerous wildlife, but it was better to be safe than sorry. Foremost, she crafted the long axe as a tool rather than a rudimentary weapon, as the hooked end acted like an extended arm to help her climb up the wreckage. There were a few bits and pieces of useless gears and broken tubing, but she was glad to find a generous length of mesh stuffed inside a holding shaft that had been attached to it by a silver ring. From the look of it, it seemed to have been a collection nozzle of some sort. At least the sheet of sheer white mesh would suffice as clothing for now. Unfortunately, it wasn't thick enough to be used as a protective tarp. Wrapping it around her waist, she used the loose metal ring to secure it.

She remembered what Valaria had told her when they had landed, as it took a while for it to hit her that the reason she continued to feel so weary was due to the thin atmosphere. Her best chance was to scout the hot desert plain after nightfall under the cool light of the stars, but that opportunity wouldn't last if Tranquility passed within the shadow of the gas giant it orbited. She had no way of knowing which way was north or south, or even what hemisphere she was on. Ala could only hope to hell that she was somewhere near where she had landed the ship. In her sketchy recollection, she recalled that there was a mountain range north of Outpost Station 9, and a great plain of dark sand to the far south.

If she could locate those areas, she figured she might at least have a chance to get her bearings. Ala tried to remember the data chart Valaria downloaded from the orbiting buoy that had marked the locations of the surrounding outposts before they had landed, but her memory was still too foggy. Ala stood upon the high dune as the second sun set upon the horizon, realizing time was of the essence. The young scavenger had to pick a direction as she weighed the options. Nobody knew she was on this desolate moon. She had come here searching for water for mere profit; now actually finding it was a matter of her own survival.

The distant sandstorms most likely meant open plains lay beyond, but the rolling clouds in the opposite direction could possibly mean a downdraft from a mountain range or valley. The thick swirling storms were enough of a deterrent for her to consider; this was a unique situation where she would have to put all her skills to the ultimate test. Hell, she would have been better off being jacked by pirates ...or maybe not. A woman had to learn to hold her own out in the void. As a spacer, she could have easily married into any colony and played the role of a housewife, where there was at least some form of decency and respect for human life. But as a privateer, any female with a decent face and a healthy body like hers was looked at merely as meat for carnal pleasure.

Ala had shoved the muzzle of her blaster in the crotch of some drunken bastard more than once, bar rooms or shipyards; it didn't make nary a difference. You even get some pretty hardcore lesbian dykes chasing the scent of pussy whenever it passed their way. She couldn't really blame them for being sick of the choice of men wandering this side of the galaxy, most males would get a hard-on staring at a dark hole in the side of a wall; it was pretty pathetic, really. Sex droids were once a hot item among the lower class spacers, but the over abused female pleasure droids had some serious mechanical problems and would malfunction from time to time in very painful and quite 'dismembering' ways.

Night fell and the stars that speckled the sky above were bright enough to see by. She had to take it slow across the desert sands, as she was weak from the lack of sufficient oxygen. Ala's options were few, she simply had to find her ship or the closest outpost so she could triangulate her location. If she could tap into the buoy frequency, she might even be able to contact the AI on the Valkyrie so it could come retrieve her. Her run of luck hadn't been so great thus far, so she wasn't going to hold her breath …besides, the air here was too thin for that anyway.

In the dark, Ala couldn't tell how far she had walked as the miles dragged on and on; the dunes eventually gave way to barren stretches of rock and boulders that littered the landscape. Every so often she would stumble across a manufactured metal plate or gear, as a testimony that humans had once been here …but were now gone and had left their trash strewn across this barren moon. Ala couldn't tell if she was hallucinating, but more than once she thought she had spotted a glimmer of light upon the horizon. It was there, then gone. Maybe it was just the starlight reflecting off something in the distance, but it was worth inspecting. Wearily, Ala decided to head in the direction of this strange beacon.

Her feet were sore and bleeding in spots, but the dry sand quickly caked within the wounds. The polearm was heavy but doubled as a walking stick of sorts. As Ala approached the area where she had seen the lights, she could hear an odd whistling noise that sounded like infrequent chirps echoing through the wind. For the life of her, she couldn't figure out what was making the unusual sound, nor could she tell their direction within the errant gales that buffeted the desert floor.

Now sure of what she had seen, Ala saw the twinkling light again coming from a dark object in the distance. It appeared there was a structure at the foot of a rocky alcove where many large stones balanced delicately on pillars of wind-blown rock; a type of natural formation for the area considering the amount of sand and wind that coursed through this part of the desert.

As she got closer, the building appeared to be multiple silos built side by side, closely connected. Several pipes ran from one section to the next. Ala had to take care where she stepped as there was a great deal of shattered debris lying about: jagged lumps of steel she couldn't quite make out in the darkness. At least this was something worth inspecting and hopefully she could find a doorway inside or equipment to make use of.

Feeling her way alongside a high wall, she came to a sudden halt as she heard a loud clang of metal fall heavily to the ground beyond the curve of a tall silo. Ala froze with her back against the steel wall as a small droid suddenly zipped through the air past her wailing in fear. A small light on its faceplate lit up the area for a brief moment as it passed her, oblivious to her presence. Another loud crash and a bright flash of light came from the opposite direction from where the small bot had fled. Considering the unknown, prudence dictated that she should follow in the direction of the fleeing droid.

It took several minutes of careful searching until she found an open chute, its door missing from its hinges. She found an attached ladder that only descended a few feet to a landing comprised of a rusted grate floor. As her eyes adjusted to the darkness within, she noticed it was only a dead end. There were several valves and broken dials and levers decorating the surrounding walls, all encrusted with rust and sand. Ala heard a rattle overhead, and jumped back when the small bot floating above peered down at her, lighting the room for a brief

Michel Savage

second with its single glowing eye.

Alarmed, it rushed towards the doorway once again, and Ala thought about grabbing for it. There was always the possibility of some kind of communication device installed in its framework, and obviously its power core was still functional; which she could certainly make use of. Maybe it had a solar pack or a redundant battery, either way she figured she could tinker with it to serve her needs. As it was about to slip beyond her reach, the bot stopped at the edge of the doorway giving a sudden pause; while making a low buzzing noise as if it were confused as to what to do. Through the open portal, Ala quickly came to realize the cause of the little bot's indecisiveness.

She almost couldn't believe what she was seeing, something that appeared to be a gigantic animal was moving between the silos. Its glowing red eyes scanned the area in front of the door. Following the droid's reaction, Ala retreated back into the shadows out of sight from the observant beast. This planet had some pretty nasty sized wildlife, but what was hard to comprehend was the metal on metal grating sound as it made its way past them. The small robot's light dimmed as it hovered there, shaking in the corner of the room, apparently quite frightened.

Ala moved slowly so that the droid wouldn't bolt out of the doorway, revealing their hiding place; and sat in the corner waiting for the creature outside to pass. She figured this was as good a place as any to get some rest until daylight came, whenever that might be. The droid seemed reluctant to be near her, but also appeared to realize that Ala wasn't a threat; or at least a lesser threat than the monstrosity lurking outside. It buzzed nervously but quietly, twitching its optical lamp.

She wondered for a long moment how this small droid could have endured intact all this time on its own, but figured it was possible. The solar collectors back at Outpost 9 had still been functional, so it seemed logical that a droid or two might have survived after all this time; as unlikely as it was. She had never seen a robot like it, let alone one that used magnetic repulsors on such a scale that would fit into its small cylindrical shell.

It was barely waist-high, with spotted metal showing under flakes of white paint. It had one retractor arm with a grasping claw that was clearly busted, along with several other compartments that appeared to be rusted shut. A few loose wires seemed to be stuffed in its neck connection with its domed head that had been fitted with a sun visor. In the dim light from its lamp, Ala could make out small lettering lining its rim: R–E–V...

"Revo Corporation," she whispered out loud to herself; the bot responded in turn as if in recognition of her words. Outside the small doorway, they could still hear the beast moving about, so she tried to be quiet, and the small droid seemed to be distinctly aware of that fact. Wanting to take a closer look at the bot, Ala tried to communicate with it; hoping its circuits weren't damaged beyond repair. Holding out her hand, it seemed apprehensive to trust her gesture to come closer.

"Your arm attachment seems to be broken, I can fix that for you," she offered quietly, so as not to attract the creature outside. With a sad buzz, the bot looked at its damaged claw and back at the girl, as if agreeing with her analysis. With a slight internal struggle, a rusted compartment on the side of the bot popped open, and a small metal tool fell to the grated floor with a loud clang.

They both froze for a tense moment as red light flashed through the open doorway at their accidental noise, but the beast slowly moved away after not sensing any movement.

The bot looked down helplessly at the tool lying on the floor, illuminating the area enough for Ala to retrieve it. It was a badly rusted wrench, but still usable. Cautiously, the droid drifted nearer, testing its own lack of trust. Ala wanted to take a closer look at this odd robot anyhow, and it was desirable to get it to cooperate willingly. As she inspected its rusted shell, Ala notice the hinge pin on the extendable arm was snapped in half. The small droid gave a worried buzz as the young girl handled it.

"*Shhh*," Ala warned, "we don't want that thing outside to hear you." At that, it immediately hushed its noise. Searching about the room Ala found a small bit of metal and bent the edges with the wrench. Without any proper synthetic lubricants available, she spit upon the fabricated pin to fit it within the hinge and attached the thumb of the claw back into place. With a squeak, the robot moved its arm and tested its claw with clear delight. Apparently, Ala had made a friend.

On the back of the bot she found more lettering, which revealed this was a soil analysis droid, or had been at one time. Though it couldn't speak, she had never seen a droid with such a distinct personality, if that's what you could call it; but perhaps it was just a programming flaw or its core circuitry going haywire from lack of maintenance over all these years and she was just imagining things. That was definitely a possibility, since she was also beginning to feel nauseous and dizzy from the lack of food and water combined with the thin air.

They both waited there in the dark for some time before the tired girl eventually passed out from exhaustion.

When she awoke, Ala wasn't too surprised to find that the small bot had disappeared; the dim light shining in through the portal told her morning had finally come. The metal grate floor was painfully cold, and she had to gather her strength to get up and take a cautious peek outside the doorway. All was quiet, and it appeared that giant beast had departed as well. The odd chirping she had heard the previous night was now silent, replaced by the light breeze whistling through the countless pipes and ducts connecting the silos.

Still blurry from the previous eve, as Ala stepped out into the morning light something caught her immediate attention. The metal plates lying around the structure she had thought were nothing more than bits of scrap, appeared strangely formed. She found more than half a dozen of them donning ribbed metal shells with pincers on the tips of thin steel legs. Their faceplates were oddly contorted with several optical lenses of multiple sizes and adorned with steel mandibles. Ala had never seen anything like it before, for all intents, it looked as if they had been intentionally fabricated to resemble beetles. If it was a joke, it didn't make any sense; why would the colonist's waste time and limited resources designing their worker droids to resemble insects?

Michel Savage

Scavengers

Searching around the silos, Ala was hoping to find a working terminal or data interface. Even without a power source or solar collector, at the very least she could salvage any spare parts she might need to bring with her. Far overhead, the REVO Corporate logo on the side of the steel building was broken and faded; miles of piping led from one silo to the next, which intersected and apparently led to an empty slab. Oddly, all the lines ended in crimped shreds, as if something had violently ripped the building that once stood there from its very foundations and hauled it away.

The young scavenger went back to inspect the odd bug-like droids that lay scattered along the edge of the silos. Their design was unique, but she couldn't find any maintenance hatches to access their interior wiring. What she didn't fail to notice though, was that these broken droids seemed to be in far better condition than the surrounding buildings that had been left abandoned. Each one of the small metallic beetles had a smoothly curved letter "**S**" branded on its side. For the life of her, Ala couldn't imagine what practical use there would be to attach hooked mandibles to a droid.

Several had their legs torn from their bodies, but every single one bore a jagged gash of one sort or another through its thick metal shell. There was no way to pry a damaged area open to take a better look inside without the risk of cutting herself, and she didn't want to take the chance of getting injured in her current weakened condition. Ala was already starting to feel sapped of energy and knew that time was running short for her if she was going to survive this. Raising a hand to shade her eyes from the harsh light, Ala looked out across the open desert she had crossed before the 2nd sun began to rise. Strong winds churned up wisps of dust across the rolling sea of sand. These silos had been built at the edge of a cleft of rocky strata; which wouldn't be difficult to climb and happened to be the highest plateau in the area, so she figured she should get up top to get a view of the terrain before the twin suns began to bake the landscape. Ala didn't want to waste another day withering away in the shade while she waited for nightfall to come, so the young scavenger started picking her way up towards the rocky summit.

The thin air was tapping her strength, and her bare feet were taking the worst of it. The material of the white mesh she had made into a skirt was simply too thin and fragile to be made into strips to wrap her feet, and would be torn to shreds in no time. Gingerly, Ala made her way over the barren rocks, taking her makeshift axe along just in case she ran into something unpleasant. Coming to rest at the edge of the summit, the sky opened up before her across an alien landscape. Purple and yellow clouds drifted lazily on the distant horizon, and below the ridge lay a vast maze of pillared rocks; much like the ones she had seen at the base of the hill near the silos. However, on this side of the plateau there were vast fields of these wind-carved columns of stone. Many of them had large boulders precariously resting atop them made of denser rock; sculpted by time at the hand of the relentless winds.

Ala made her way down within the shadow of the hillside into the labyrinth of sand and stone. It was only when she had reached the base that she began to notice tracks in the dirt; parallel markings on the ground that could have very well been made by the metallic beetles she had seen. The size of the strange footprints was consistent with the spacing of their legs. Ala figured it would only be prudent to follow their tracks back to the source. She had seen dozens of terraforming projects in her time as a spacer, from claustrophobic domed units to expensive grand projects left completely abandoned from lack of both funds and labor; but planet-wide terraforming was another breed all to itself. The amount of currency involved was staggering, but allowed the corporate benefactor sole claim to all of the ore and mineral rights. Then they could rape the planet through low-cost surface mining and make their investment back several-fold by selling off the resources to whoever could pay the transport fees.

From what she had heard, it was the lowly colonists who slaved away on these projects who got the short end of the deal. They would give a decade or more of their lives to the corporate benefactor for a small plot of land to call their own, only to find their new homeworld was being stripped down around them. Mega Corporations didn't care about people they hired to do the dirty work; they only cared about reaping the profits. To them, dreamy-eyed settlers were only a tool. Ala could see that fact a parsec away, and she never understood why other spacers would waste so much of their short lives chasing an empty dream.

The human race had a planet of their own once, and we fucked it up the ass without hesitation. Ala remembered flipping through the digital fairytale images of old Earth when she was just a child; she guessed that was the age when she started hating people in general. It was hard to believe the Eden we once lived in and how they razed it to the ground; turning it into such a polluted crap hole that nobody wanted to live there anymore. So here we were, the majority of mankind scattered among the stars chasing what we had lost.

The REVO Corporation must have had a reason for choosing this moon over so many other worlds, which were far closer to the major space lanes. The young pilot was still regretting not having taken the time to study the buoy data before rushing off to get her ass planet-side. Then again, Ala wasn't exactly famous for her patience; that was something she would certainly have to work on if she survived this escapade. She followed the tracks out among the forest of stones when a distant rumbling caught her attention. Ala heard a rush of shifting sand behind her and spun around, but the noise had suddenly stopped.

Still suspicious, she gripped the steel bar that was her axe even tighter and continued on her way; following the ever fading trail of footprints in the dirt. Looming clouds rolled in the distance as she made her way across the valley floor. They were thick and gloomy like the wall of an approaching sandstorm. After pondering if she should make her way back to the silos for shelter, Ala finally admitted to herself she was living on borrowed time and didn't have more than a day or two at best to find water and something to eat before she would collapse. Over the ridge beyond a thick haze stood a forest of strange enormous formations, vast domed mountains that spanned out like an umbrella over thin structures of stone that somehow supported their weight.

Likely they were carved by the frequent low level sandstorms that blanketed this region. Still, one would think that such formations would take eons to create. Ala was also curious to see what this solitary moon had looked like before the catastrophe which had engulfed the planet. Maybe it hadn't been a reactor malfunction after all; something as simple as a meteor shower or a cataclysmic flux in the ionosphere that turned the weather patterns sour; magnetic eruptions from the core or any number of solar events could cause a substantial amount of grief to anyone living upon the surface.

Ala was thinking out loud just to keep her mind off how exhausted she was, and decided to take a seat in the shade under one of the stone pillars. She was wiping the sweat from her brow when she heard that odd sound of sifting sand behind her again. Peering around the edge of the rock, she saw nothing unusual as the noise subsided. Sitting on the bedrock above the sandy silt of the valley floor, her eyes widened as a huge lump of sand lifted into a mound and fell back to the ground; creating the same noise she had heard before. Something was lurking beneath the surface, and it had been following her!

The young spacer assumed anything that could displace that much soil must be big, very big. Considering the size of the beast with the glowing eyes that had kept her cowering through the night, maybe the native wildlife of this small planet tended to be on the larger side of the scale. Throughout the galaxy, where mankind has invaded one planet or another, there was a far higher percentage of flora opposed to animal life to be found. Some creatures were just mere blobs of jelly and countless others that were just as uninteresting. She couldn't recall, however, of any record of an alien species that could survive in the same atmosphere and pressure which humans required to sustain themselves.

Ala slowly got down upon one knee, wondering how this thing was burrowing through the subsurface. Further away, the sand erupted again for but a moment, and she caught a silver glean that reflected the sunlight from beneath the shifting grains of sand. As she turned to her left, Ala nearly jumped out of her skin when she came face to face with the small droid she had encountered the night before. Apparently, the little bot had snuck up on her without making a sound. It gave a short buzz as its eye twisted around, dimming its optics; if that was a hint to keep silent, Ala wasn't about to argue.

Another mound of sand erupted, though now much further in the distance. Had the small bot been trailing her all this time? Here in the daylight she could see it much more clearly, its grasping claw she had repaired was still functional. It was far more battered and in worse shape than the girl had first noticed; there were numerous small holes melted into its shell, which itself was rusting apart. Bare wires seemed to have been crudely mashed into place around the swivel on its neck joint. It also seemed to have several other nonfunctional attachments hanging below its embedded magnetic repulsor cups that were lining its undercarriage.

The floating canister seemed to look at her with mild interest, and Ala was wishing there was a way they could properly communicate. Hoping its chip for voice recognition was intact after thirty years in this abusive environment, she wearily tried to open a dialog.

"Look, I don't know if you actually have any voice perception hardware in that tin can of yours, so let's just keep this simple," Ala stated with a sigh as the droid turned its attention back to her, "…buzz once for yes, and twice for no; got it?"

She truly wasn't expecting an answer, but after a long moment of the droid seeming to be concentrating on linking the words of her question; it finally buzzed once and was silent. She took that as a good sign.

"So ...you *do* understand me?"

"*Bzzzt*." The bot responded with a higher tone, its one large optical eye looking back at her. The young girls tongue was becoming swollen and her lips were now parched, and her stomach was slowly turning into knots. Hunger was beginning to claw at her; at least she was in decent physical shape and would last longer than most people in this situation. Still, things were looking pretty desperate as they were.

"I don't know why you're following me, but it seems like we're both in this mess together," which was more of an observation than a statement as Ala stood up and peered out over the alien horizon. Looking back at the droid, it was clear it also had the traits of a survivor, or programming peripherals along that line that had kept it running this long on its own. That was something useful in these circumstances.

"I need water ...H_2O; do you know where to find it?" She inquired with a measure of hope. To her relief, it responded with a single buzz, yes, "And this source of water is nearby?" Only after the droid took a long moment to contemplate her question as it gazed off in the direction of the looming mountains in the distance, until it finally turned back and offered a positive response. Still, that little pause worried her.

"Can you take me there?" She asked, and again, it agreed. At least this was some sort of progress, though that giant sand mole or whatever it was lurking beyond the edge of the bedrock, still troubled her. Floating casually over the terrain, the small droid began to head off slowly towards the distant pillared plateau of the mountain range. Ala became jealous of the droid's ease of mobility. She would have happily straddled its shell for a free ride, but she also noted that the bot was solely designed for minimal weight and was likely capable of only carrying a few extra pounds, if that.

She had seen such robotic units from time to time on other colonies, though they came in widely diverse designs. They were used to scout the land and harsh terrain, and take remote soil samples, test pH levels and whatnot. Such drones would be put to extensive use during the initial terraforming process on new worlds, but were still widely used in agricultural industries where open swaths of land were utilized instead of soil-less hydroponics gardens. Changing the atmosphere to breathable air was relatively easy compared to making alien topsoil friendly for Terran plants. Without the proper balance of nitrates, earth-type plants simply won't thrive. Then, of course, temperature and O^2 levels have a lot to do with it, so they usually ended up having to genetically adapt the plants to coexist with the alien environment. She couldn't pretend to know all the complicated details; personally, Ala hated everything to do with farming.

Though she was wary to keep an ear out for the creature lurking in the sand dunes, she did note that the bot was considerate enough to spin its head around back towards her from time to time, to make sure she was keeping up with it. There were several areas where her pace was slowed as the weary girl had to scramble up wide boulders and narrow clefts between the canyons that dotted the rough terrain that stretched between them and the mountains. As the miles dragged on following the path of the droid, she was beginning to lose patience as no sign of a riverbed, nor spring, or reservoir was in sight. Apparently, the robot's definition of 'close by' was not measured in human footsteps.

Ala kept scanning the horizon for another outpost tower or deserted station for her salvation, yet there was nothing. Her feet were sore and scraped from the long trek, and the bladed hook she had made seemed to become a heavier burden with every step. Within its eccentric orbit around the twin suns, the parent gas giant slipped below the mountain range as the suns began to follow in its wake. The long shadow of the curiously shaped plateaus began to sweep over their trail as the bot continued to head directly towards the base of one of these bizarre monoliths. These strange mountains stood like mutated mushrooms as the upper portion fanned out above the thin rocky skeleton of its supporting base.

"Wait right there, rust bucket," Ala muttered angrily as she came to a stop, the fatigue of chasing after this hovering can of bolts had shortened her fuse considerably, "You said this place was close by, you lying bastard," she fumed, as the robot floated back to her. Trying to catch her breath in this thin air was nearly impossible, and she noticed for a brief moment that the droids robotic claw was touching her hair with profound curiosity as she was leaning over in exhaustion.

"I see your arm is still working…" Ala grumbled out loud, wondering why the droid was showing interest in her hair. It buzzed once in response, as it retracted its arm away; spinning the claw and clicking it open and shut in gleeful display until something in the mechanism crimped, and the motorized claw jammed. The robot gave a worried buzz as it gave a sad look at its once again broken pincer. Despite her mood, Ala had to laugh.

"Well, that's what you get for showing off," she taunted, but like a tormented child, the bot only gave a mournful whine in response.

"Really though, bullshit aside; I need to know how far we have to go to get there ...to this water supply of yours," she demanded as the robot floated away towards its original path momentarily, then came back; only to reply with a long string of high and low buzzing tones.

"Look, I don't know what you're trying to say, so just give it a rest!" Ala spouted at the blank face droid, "I'm not here for the scenic tour, how far away is it? One, two, five kilometers ...how many?" To answer, the bot took a long moment to respond with three notes.

"Three, just three kilometers ...are you sure?" She had to ask, the bot responded with its single tone; *yes*. With a shrug, Ala gave the little bot the benefit of the doubt, as this particular class of droids usually worked in grids and were fairly accurate in that function at least. Then again, three decades in this dry desolation could have baked its circuits for all she knew.

At least in the cool shadows of these strange mountains they were out of the searing heat. It made the girl wonder why the engineers of the Avalon project chose this particular location on the lunar plain considering the twin stars beating down upon it, however, she could imagine this climate would be far more tolerable with decent cloud cover. Had they completed the terraforming process, the atmosphere would have been decently breathable and converted the water they were pumping from the underground aquifers into the condenser towers above each moisture silo to create the clouds.

It was an extremely complicated process to replicate Mother Nature, but damn well profitable when it was done right. Ala did wonder though, how any native wildlife would adapt to such drastic changes to the pressure and climate, or if they just died off as hapless victims of the process. Her head began to hurt thinking about it, a sign of severe dehydration. Stumbling along, they made their way over several deep ravines stretched together by precarious bridges of rock. The little droid had no issues floating over these hazardous obstacles with ease, but there path crossed several deep drops that put its two-legged companion at mortal risk.

As they neared the narrow base of one particular mountain, the sprouting of strangely hued aquamarine and crimson foliage became more abundant along their path. Under the enormous umbrella of rock, cooler temperatures allowed these plants to thrive. She had seen a great deal of alien vegetation in her time, but couldn't recognize any of these species. Some appeared like bubbly moss and others like hairy stems, others were simply downright indescribable. Hopefully, plants meant the presence of water; but on an alien world, it might not mean squat.

The droid ran off with determination, and Ala could finally tell where it was heading. A small ridgeline opened into a sharp cleft carved within the strata to what appeared to be a natural cave formation. The interior was actually much larger than it looked from the outside, which was partially hidden by its location. The small cavity wasn't terribly deep, and there was still several hours of sunlight left that radiated into the shallow cave. A collection of scrap metal and pieces of machinery lined the walls within. Odds and ends from transport shuttles and shielding panels, along with countless gears and tubing lay stacked or strewn about the secluded grotto.

Upon closer inspection, the girl noticed the bits and pieces were set in particular order or aligned with one another based on either color or size. It made her wonder if there were survivors living here, no matter how remote that possibility might be. Then again, Ala wasn't exactly thinking straight at this point as lightheaded as she was.

"Hello ...is there anyone here?" She choked out from her dry throat, not really expecting an answer. The bot, which had disappeared into the back of the cave, reappeared again, and was carrying a large clunky gear in its grasping claw. It looked at Ala for a mere second, then hovered away over to one of the arrangements of scrap, and carefully put the gear in place thoughtfully, delicately, as if it were putting together a puzzle.

Well, so much for getting her hopes up; it was now apparent this bot had spent a great deal of time on its hobby as a collector. Old bits of rusted metal and plating, some far larger than she would have thought the small droid was capable of carrying, were leaned up against both walls of the single room cave.

"Hey, you bucket of bolts, I really need that water!"

Like a kid caught screwing around who hadn't done his chores, the bot turned about with a look of guilt. After a brief pause of indecisiveness, the bot drifted off into the shadows at the back of the cave once again. With a creak of metal, a huge panel leaning against the far wall tipped up and over, crashing to the floor with a flutter of dust. Behind it floated the droid, who promptly pointed to the metal cask propped above it. Plastered upon the side of the vat was the familiar REVO company logo, plastered above an attached water spout.

Ala walked over to the container and gave it a few sharp knocks, the resounding echo revealed that it was nearly full as water sloshed inside. She couldn't believe it, there must have been more than a thousand gallons in there. The real question was if it was still safe to drink after all this time? With the little strength she had left, Ala tipped over a dented section of hull plating in effort to keep the precious liquid from draining into the sand of the cave floor. Braced as it was high above her reach, she instructed the robot to release the valve. The droid hovered over to the spout and used its clamp tool to spin the lock.

In all honesty, she was expecting it to be either infested with alien bacteria or entirely tainted with rust …but as it turned out, the REVO Corporation must have been using high-grade tanks. Clear water dribbled out into her hands, washing away the layer of dust coating her skin. It didn't take much effort for her to dare to take a sip. If it was stale, her dry throat certainly couldn't tell at this point. There were bacterial filters lining the interior tank walls; as valuable as water was to the colonists, every effort was made to keep their storage silos sterile.

Noticing how she was consuming the water, the droid continued to rotate the valve, releasing a stream to shower down upon her. Days before, Ala would have been frantic over such an expensive waste of water, but it felt so good in her dehydrated condition that she bathed under it, washing away the dirt, sweat and soil. Squandering a few dozen gallons was worth the sensation of being alive at this point. Even dirtied, the wastewater could be filtered once again if she found something to seal it in. The droid just fluttered there, watching Ala with interest as she bathed naked in the fading light.

Staring down at the tub of muddied water, she shrugged off the twinge of guilt. One thing her father had taught her well was the ability to brush off the feeling of regret. "*You are where you are*," was his motto; even at the times they were living in squalor, it was his humble way of showing his daughter a measure of self-dignity and helping her to hold her head high, despite their poverty. Over time, Ala came to understand what he had truly meant; that no matter where you were or what curves and hardships life has thrown your way; that you had to keep believing in yourself. Though she never again heard him repeat those words after his wife died in the station tragedy, it was as if his own proverb had somehow lost its luster. He was never the same man after that.

Still, her father's words haunted her on every salvage job she pulled. It was sad and difficult at times to witness the aftermath of countless lost lives and the air sucked out of the hopes and dreams of those unfortunate pioneers who were only guilty of searching for a better life, only to be taken by the vacuum of space or some other tragic mishap planet-side. You had to be emotionally strong to make it as a scavenger; otherwise you'd go nuts asking yourself the purpose of it all. "*Keep trying, no matter the odds…*" her mother, Valaria, would always say. It took Ala many years to realize just how alike both her parents had truly been.

The cool winds blowing into the cavern dried her wet body. The setting suns were taking their time casting long double shadows across the landscape far beyond the rocky cliffs and distant dunes. The bot buzzed around on its own errands while talking to itself as Ala rifled through the collection of junk. She eventually found the droid further back in the darkened recess of the cave, methodically arranging another pile of debris. Ala was about to ask what the hell he was doing as her eyes adjusted to the dark, but it wasn't until she had nearly bumped into the hovering bot that she actually saw what it was handling.

It turned to her once with casual indifference as it placed a dried bone in the middle of what appeared to be a macabre confusion of human skeletons. Ala's mouth dropped open in shock. What must have been the remnants of a dozen bodies, lay there in the sand; broken skulls and ribs including segments of spines were all neatly placed in an odd order, as if the bot was trying to put together a puzzle without having any clue as to how the pieces fit. As mortified as she was at the prospect this droid had been gathering human remains, she also understood that at some sublevel of programming, it was simply collecting what it may have thought was merely salvageable bits of scrap.

The piles of metal and wiring, tubing, and other assorted gears placed in rows according to size meant this strange droid was simply following some subroutine to gather salvageable parts. Now as to why a soil analysis droid would be given that instruction was beyond her comprehension. Maybe there actually had been a few lingering survivors from the Avalon project who made an effort to collect resources and held out as long as they could before they met their demise. Of course, a surveyor droid would have no idea how to put together a human skeleton, nor would it contain any ethical subroutines to keep it from collecting the dead cadavers strewn among the scattered debris left over from the decimated colony.

In all her years, Ala had seen a lot of corpses of people who died in a lot of bad ways, but nothing close to bots playing with their body parts. This was just …just wrong! As much as she wanted to walk away, Ala had to intervene.

"Stop, put that down!" She ordered, yelling at the droid who responded with what could be interpreted as a quizzical look. It dropped the femur it had been holding, where it plopped to the ground, and then quickly reached out to turn it neatly into place at the last second. Its guilt was obvious, as the bot retracted its clamp-arm instantly when Ala took an angry step forward.

"Don't touch these ever again!" She yelled while taking a step in front of the droid, while making sure that it heard and would obey the command. The bot backed away fearfully in momentary confusion, then swerved off towards the entrance. Shaking her head with disbelief, Ala made her way back to the piles of metal salvage; hoping she could find some functioning electronics in the piles of junk. She was beginning to wonder what she was going to do for nourishment, and faintly remembered a children's tale she had once heard about 'Bone Soup', which was a pretty sick parody at this particular moment.

Searching through the electronics and machinery, she came across a light scribe in a spare compartment. Even though the bot was now noticeably avoiding her and keeping a respectable distance, Ala ordered it over to where she was sitting, and timidly, it obeyed.

"Look here, you're my only friend at the moment and I didn't mean to scare you off like that," she confessed, then began laughing at herself for apologizing to a machine, but quickly realized her life was on the line here, and she couldn't afford to have the droid perceive her as a threat on any level. She certainly didn't cherish the thought of her own bones being placed among that morbid pile in the not so distant future.

"I fixed your hand, remember?" Ala reminded the bot as it turned its eye and clacked its clamp once in deep thought, "If I can find a translator around here, I'll install you with a voice box, but in the meantime, we really need to give you a name." At that suggestion, the bot buzzed in agreement.

The light scribe ended up not working so well, as it was intended, but she found a sealed container of grease stain and used it to paint on the side of the droid in big letters, then used the UV beam from the light scribe to cure it.

"There you go, B.O.B," she finished, wiping the stain from her fingers, "Bob, stands for *Bucket of Bolts*," Ala grinned to herself. She couldn't tell if 'BoB' approved of his new designation by his response, but the name was going to stick whether he liked it or not.

Questions

The mixed collection of spare parts and metal sheeting were a far cry from anything a recycling crew would collect. Equipment grabbed planet-side would have to be dismantled before being loaded into a storage hold. On many occasions, derelict ships left floating in space were much easier to handle and required only towing into an open bay aboard an orbital station. There was once a time when these cadavers were actually kept by the scavy's and sold back to their grieving kindred at a steep price. In some circumstances, that barter was grossly abused whenever it was discovered that the remains belonged to a family of any considerable wealth, and such valuable corpses were ransomed off for their return.

When certain financial entrepreneurs began to get scent of that scam, criminal enterprises soon followed in their wake. Both common spacers and the governing laws began cracking down on anyone trafficking human remains for a price; a general edict granted that their ships or terrestrial property could be seized by any local settlers or colonists. Now, whenever salvagers found a score, it was only prudent to dispose of any bodies into space by giving them a nudge towards the nearest star or leaving them to rot on the planet where they were found.

But the situation here on Tranquility still left Ala baffled. The only reason she could think that this planet was left abandoned for the past three decades was that the REVO Corp had gone belly up. Recovering the materials and resources would cost a bundle of time and credits, but it certainly would have been worth the investment by any corporate competitor to salvage. Ala truly didn't know what the interstellar corporations had on contract laws; perhaps they were barred from touching another business's terrestrial claim, even if it was abandoned. Still, that's exactly where Scavenger crews fit in; filling in the shades of gray that shadowed property rights of individual spacers and colonists, corporate or otherwise.

She could understand if all records of the Avalon project here on Tranquility had been lost over time, but the chattering from those two old-timers back on Pandora proved that argument moot.

Ala stepped outside to view the twin sunsets on this forgotten alien world; several more of the colossal mushroom-shaped mountains dotted the horizon, casting their eerie shadows across the landscape. She could only hope that somewhere in all this debris littering the cavern floor that there might be some working electronics she could rewire to help her find her ship; otherwise, she was going to be hard up for food if there weren't any condensed emergency rations hiding somewhere in all of this mess. Chances were against that on every level.

The sky turned a purple hue dashed with strings of red as the larger of the twin suns dipped below the horizon. Her estimate was the smaller of the two suns was following an hour or so behind it. Shielding her eyes, Ala observed a cloud drifting from an adjacent peak. It swirled in formation, and she noticed the cloud was made of tiny specs. She watched as another cloud emerged from the shadow beneath another peak farther in the distance, swirling like the other as the cloud suddenly dispersed and fanned out across the evening sky.

Taking a few steps further outside the grotto, she looked

up to see if the same aerial display was forming from the underside of the peak above her. The girl stood there for a long while getting a crick in her neck staring upwards to no avail. She had not been planet-side on a living world for so long that it took her a moment to remember these odd clouds resembled a flock of birds. Ala recalled seeing real ones a few times in her early childhood, however, most avian species were now only viewable on holographic videos. Had the colonist's transplanted avian life here, or were these native life forms? With her stomach growling in defiance, Ala was hoping the latter was true but realized hunger could drive one to commit some pretty stupid and reckless mistakes, which she had learned from personal experience.

BoB drifted over to where she was standing, seemingly agitated and buzzing in double-beeps, "No, no, no…" over and over again. Pushing off the annoying bot, Ala began to notice that several of these strange birds were heading in their direction and she could make out their form the closer they approached. First they appeared to have the wide wingspans of seagulls from Earth, but she knew that was a ludicrous thought as they had all gone extinct over a century ago. It took some strained thought to remember what these looked like. Then it slowly occurred to her that they appeared to resemble bats.

From what she remembered, most were so petite you could hold one in your hand, and she figured she might have to catch more than a few to make a decent meal. For the life of her, Ala couldn't recall what bats were attracted to or what she could use as bait, admitting she had failed to retain anything she had learned in school that she didn't much care about. The hard truth was, the vast majority of animal species that spacers were taught about in educational classes, they would actually never see in real life, so like most kids, Ala never really gave a shit. The only zoo's she had ever been to were nothing but museums of stuffed animals accompanied by videos and holograms of natural fauna.

One of these flying creatures was making a line straight for her, and in turn, BoB responded with a high pitched wail. Ala was shocked that the droid had the audacity to clamp her arm while giving a harsh tug. Angrily, Ala turned to pry its grasping claw off of her.

"What the hell? That hurt!" She snapped back.

It was only when she followed the bot's gaze as it turned back towards the sky that she heard the flap of enormous wings. The strange bat creature had certainly lost its perspective size against the monolithic background of the towering mountain peaks. As it got closer, she could tell this thing was much, much larger than she had first thought. With every skip of her heartbeat, the creature grew double in size. BoB froze and Ala gasped silently as the beast landed with a thud on the ground only a few dozen feet from where she stood. This was no terrestrial bat, though it was certainly bat-like.

It stood there on all fours, nearly as tall as two men. It didn't have hair as a bat would, but smooth black skin and muscular winged forearms. Its legs were small in comparison to the rest of its body, much like its terrestrial counterpart; as was its pig-like snout. Its eyes were large and red, and had a dull white glaze over them. It appeared to have no neck, although it did have two large tusks protruded from the sides of its mouth, where several rows of sharp teeth glittered from within. Oddly, though BoB and Ala could see it clearly in front of them, the creature didn't look directly at them but stood there snorting as if testing the air.

It wasn't a great feeling to suddenly realize she was the only chunk of living meat in the area. The creatures grotesquely bulging forearms rippled as it twitched its muscles while sniffing the air. In shock, Ala was momentary indecisive to choose if she should turn heel and run for the cover of the cave, not knowing if it would hear or sense her movements. As it pivoted its tusked face slowly towards the two, BoB's sad whine indicated that the jig was up; giving away any hope they had of taking the initiative.

Ala realized her paltry homemade axe with its palm wide blade would do little against such a massive beast, let alone hundreds of them should they swarm down upon her. She was assuming that BoB was also in mortal danger, forgetting this little droid had survived here on his own long before she was even born. Ala was confident in presuming the tusks and vicious teeth made this terrifying creature a carnivore, and thus, had a taste for blood. BoB had been trying to protect the girl by warning her to take cover and she had brushed him off with her usual sassy attitude; realizing she should have given the droid the benefit of the doubt and it was significantly more intelligent than she had first thought.

The girl stumbled as she spun towards the cave entrance as the beast turned its attention toward them with a snort. It used its forearms to lurch towards the pair much like an ape, dragging its web winged appendages in the sand along behind it. There were plenty of places to hide between the sheets of metal and piles of debris, but a beast of such enormous size could tear through it like so much chaff. BoB skirted a stack of plating and became very still, shifting his head nervously. It took Ala a hectic few seconds to spot a line of rusted steel piping, finding one just large enough for her to crawl into. There were a lot of sharp edges protruding from the stacks of metal, and she had to be careful not to lacerate herself.

Backing up into the pipe, she kept her pointed axe poised in front of her as she peered out of the far end. The monster thudded along, seemingly half-blind as it moved its head from side to side; sniffing the air with its flattened nostrils. She was hoping its sense of hearing was as hampered as its vision, while Ala tried to control her nervous breath. As it shuffled through the piles of junk, it sliced its wing on a protruding edge of jagged steel. Though a minor wound, it gave a loud stuttered cackle in response to the pain it was inflicted. Sniffing at the steel panel where it had received the injury, it suddenly lurched back its head, apparently repulsed by the strong scent of oxidized metal.

The beast chattered again while it received several more bloodied scrapes as it dragged its wings through the sharp debris. Ala huddled back into the recess of the pipe as far as possible when its fetid breath wafted inside the tube as it snorted overhead. Wide-eyed, she held her breath as the creature inspected the small pool of water below the tank where she had bathed; catching her scent. Although the shallow cave was fairly wide, the ceiling was not high enough for the enormous beast to unfurl its wings or become airborne. Blindly tracking the scent of flesh through this bramble of metal thorns came at a painful price.

There was a long moment of silence, and Ala was about to poke her head out of the pipe when the world outside took a violent spin. The monster had knocked down the stack of pipes in a chorus of clanging metal as they rolled out onto the cavern floor. Ala groaned from being bruised by the tumble, having failed to brace herself within the narrow tube. Lying on her back, she raised her eyes to see a heavy paw with curled talons come to rest just outside the end of the pipe. While nervously gritting her teeth, Ala wondered how she would escape this dire predicament.

There was a flash of light and the sound with a familiar report. "*Whoopissh*! *Whoopissh*!" The green mottled beam of a direct energy weapon ripped into the cave wall with a fizzled impact, the second hit a stack of metal casings; sending shrapnel bouncing off the walls, and more than a few bits rained down upon the pipe that she was in, accompanied by several loud clangs from their impacts. Outside her field of view, BoB had grabbed a functioning weapon from his stash pile of junk. The recoil of each shot left him spinning on his repulsors in a way that would almost be hilarious if it wasn't for the serious gravity of their situation. After recovering from the first blast, BoB used his claw arm to take another shot at the beast in his effort to protect Ala.

Not having the advantage of a human frame, BoB had no shoulder to rest the thick butt of the plasma rifle upon. The second shot nearly ripped his claw arm off at its joint. Luckily, the giant bat was both blinded and dazed by the discharge of the firearm, and beat its wings in alarm to escape; making a fatal mistake in doing so. Its wingspan was far too wide for the confines of the grotto as it stumbled upon the pipes and sharp metal scrap it had knocked to the floor. One beat of its powerful wings sent it reeling backward onto a spliced pipe that had come to rest at a dangerous angle, impaling the horrid creature through its broad chest.

Though large and muscular as it was, like most avian species, its bones were hollow with muscles laced over a thin skeletal frame. The steel bar met hardly any resistance as the jagged spear lanced through its body, inflicting a mortal wound. With a lurch, it kicked its small hind feet, letting off a high pitched scream that painfully climbed the decibel range to the point that Ala had to clamp her ears. Finally, a blissful silence settled with the dust as a few last remnants of scrap metal bent and toppled under the sheer weight of the beast as it expired and toppled to the ground.

Crawling out from the tube on her scraped knees, Ala passed an astonished look towards the bot who seemed just as surprised as she. His one eye shifting to her and back at the massive corpse crumpled beyond, signaling with both a worried and inquisitive beep. She waltzed over to disarm the droid who had let the gun muzzle drop safely off its target. The weapon looked like an old military issue Centurion blaster, she had seen a few owned by mercenaries in her travels. That would certainly come in handy!

"You're full of surprises I see…" she trailed off as the body of the creature shifted, and she spun with a practiced hand, rifle point to bear on its target in one fluid motion. Noting the beast was truly dead, she turned back towards the droid. A few sparks flew from where its arm joint had been twisted by the kick of the blaster. BoB gave a poutful buzz as he tested the damaged arm.

"Give me a moment, and I'll fix that," Ala promised the droid with a distracted glance towards the mouth of the cave. She gingerly tiptoed to the entrance and peered out into the evening sky, peeking up just beyond the rim of the stone roof. The swarm of giant bats had dispersed out beyond the open tundra, and thankfully, the ruckus in their little hollow had not attracted any additional unwelcome guests.

The fact was, she was starving at this point, and her stomach growled to remind her she needed to eat. Finding the cache of water was a boon, but now she needed real sustenance. Though unappealing as it was, the giant carcass of the creature was currently the only means of protein. There might be edible roots or vegetation in the surrounding area, but there was always the risk of poisoning herself. Ala, of course, was fully aware of the risks of contracting pathogens from alien species, so she wasn't about to nibble on its raw flesh.

After wasting a bit of time searching the dim cave, she found a few spare parts to repair the bot's twisted arm. She gathered some dried vegetation that resembled brush and twigs from around the entrance outside, wondering if they would even burn. Though the brush appeared something like wood, the branches had a soft fleshy interior that needed to be scraped out. The air was thin here and she knew starting a fire would be nearly impossible, so she experimented with the rifle to see if she could cheat somehow.

Blasters and plasma rifles were dangerous enough to handle as they were, but she knew this one had been lying around for over three decades without any form of routine maintenance. There were restrictor coils within the gun that held the plasma charge, which were commonly guaranteed to last a lifetime; that is, forty years or so in real time. However, that was considering if it was kept clean and in good repair. Like gunpowder cannons of old, any kind of decay in the housing could cause it to crack and explode, which would be substantially worse when one was dealing with energized plasma.

Ala knew better than to tempt fate, and decided against breaching the rusted casing to surgically adjust it the way she had done before with her old hand blaster. Energy weapons were especially nasty. If the restrictor coils snapped while she was handling it, the resulting flash of raw plasma would melt anything together; flesh, metal, or bone would fuse in an instant. They made for some pretty horrific wounds. All in all, it was still a heat beam. Though the grit of sand scraped within the dial, she turned down the setting to the lowest point. After setting a length of steel bar upright, crossing her fingers, she put the muzzle near its tip and pulled the trigger.

The shot engulfed the bar and continued out the cave mouth, violently kicking up a pile of dirt from the ground outside. The tip of the bar remained glowing red hot, and she only had a few seconds to spare as she grabbed it by the cooler end and stuffed it into the pile of twigs. After a few moments of gentle blowing, to her delight, she got a spark to flame. This alien wood did not burn terribly well and let off thick smoke with a distinct greenish tint, but it would serve to cook her paltry meal of bat steak.

As the second sun began to sink over the horizon, Ala sliced open the dead carcass with her sharpened blade. Its skin was incredibly thin, too thin for being tanned and made into something useful like shoes or clothing. The most disgusting part was that its blood was oddly translucent, and its muscles had a yellowish taint to it making it even more unappealing. Cutting apart a few slabs and placing it on a hand-made spit over the fire, Ala's stomach grumbled loudly. BoB seemed to be amazed at her efforts to create customized fuel for herself and buzzed around the cave with intent interest at what she was doing while he observe the process.

Sitting down beside the fire, tired and bruised, Ala took a timid bite into her first meal in days. It tasted like salted soy pork with a distinctly sour aftertaste. As repulsive as it was, having been without food for so long, she wolfed it down with a good measure of water as a chaser. After a bit of rest and getting her strength back, Ala opened her sleepy eyes to see the droid placing fresh wood fuel into the fire. She was quite amazed at that small act of concern, for she had not instructed the bot to do so; the little droid was clearly acting on its own reconnaissance.

"Apparently, there's more to you than meets the eye," she stated gently as she eased her self back up. Watching the bot buzz off and return with a few more twigs of firewood, which it clumsily set down with its twisted arm, Ala remembered her promise, "Come over here Bob, and let's fix that, shall we," she motioned to the droid as she fumbled through spare parts she had brought within the cone of light from their small fire.

She experienced a moment of deja vu as she sat there tinkering with the metal in the dim firelight, drifting in from outside came a sound she had almost forgotten. She got up to walk to the mouth of the cave to inspect the source of the strange noise; the calming song of crickets. A flood of memories of her parents during her childhood erupted from nowhere, wrapping her mind in a blanket of tearful emotions.

She slowly returned back to the fireplace as BoB gave an inquisitive whine. Had she been space-bound for so long that she had forgotten the sound of nature, the gust of a fresh breeze or the feeling of sunlight upon her skin?

Whatever the catastrophe that had befallen this accursed moon all those decades ago, these insects had survived it. Just like on earth when most other animal species died away, the insects had always found a way to thrive.

Concentrating on the job at hand, after a bit of tinkering and a one-sided conversation, she had fixed the droid's arm with a woven wire brace; making it even more robust than before. Picking up the rifle, she displayed it to the eager droid.

"Bob, do you have any more of these firearms in storage?" She asked softly. The droid's eye shifted left and right for a moment and put its one claw hand up to its faceplate in a very human-like way as if in thought, then turned around and buzzed off into the dark shadows of the cavern. After a great deal of noise from clanging and shifting of metal that echoed from the distant gloom beyond the reach of the dim firelight, the small droid reappeared, dragging an armful of relics in its wake.

As the bot eagerly dropped them down next to the fire, Ala could see that some weren't even guns at all, but were merely gun-shaped pieces of machinery. Within the mess she found an old low-magnum hand blaster that was quite broken, and a twisted stun weapon that seemed to have been salvaged from a prison ship, and one other Centurion blaster that was so mashed up it was only held together by bits of torn metal. All the time the droid was buzzing on incomprehensibly about something, but of course, she didn't understand a damn word of it.

The girl realized that she would have to find a speech box or hand-held voice receptor so she could resolve this communications issue with the droid. As of now, she had survived another day and at least had food in her belly, and water to drink but she did worry how long it would take before the bat's carcass would begin to putrefy. Those creatures seemed to have a honed sense of smell, yet had a notable aversion to the scent of oxidized metal; which was something she might use to her advantage the young scavenger thought to herself while inspecting the firearms.

"What I really need is a way to determine our location, a nav-com or any kind of mapping device," Ala trailed off in thought as BoB gave a quizzical buzz, "...even a communications board might do. Is there anything like that in these piles of junk?"

At first, the bot gave a sad whine, then perked up for a moment as something hit his memory banks. As he flitted off to one side of the cavern, Ala grabbed a torch from the fire to follow the droid into the darkness. BoB floated about dropping broken digital tablets and other useless bits of garbage at her feet; at last he stopped at a wall of stacked metal. Peering behind it with the torch, Ala saw something that put a smile on her face. It was far too heavy to move the plates of steel, so she grabbed a metal bar to lever the thick panels away from the wall. With a grunt of exhaustion, the steel hull plating teetered and fell with a crash to the floor.

Revealed behind it was a small ejection pod, likely once used on an industrial excavation or transport vehicle. Bots were usually used for such menial labor with simple programmed instructions to haul materials from site A to B, etc. Though, many were still fitted with a human interface board and seat so they could be piloted when needed. This one seemed in pretty damn good condition. It was just a detached pod though, with nothing else linked. Ala still wondered how all this equipment and scrap metal came to be located in this solitary cave far from any visible settlements.

The rusted top hatch took a little effort to pry open, but with a pop, the seal finally came free. There was only a sparse amount of dust coating the seat within so she was hoping that the rest of the electronics inside had not been compromised. Salvation was at hand if she could get this gizmo up and running. In short order, she found the battery sling. It was a long row of slots where chip cores were inserted for power, though it was entirely empty except for one. There were five of the six slots left to fill before she could hope to get this thing online. With a little struggle, she pulled the sole battery chip out and showed it to the bot.

"Bob, I need several more of these," she pointed to the metal card; waving it in front of his red eye to analyze, "get me anything that looks like this that you might have around here," She ordered. The bot floated off to rifle through its collection of junk and debris while Ala familiarized herself with the console.

It was usually the work of artists that made great advances in technology available. Radioactive materials were generally used as long-lasting sources of power but their applications were always complicated, until someone with a creative mind came up with the idea to slice up paper-thin wafers of Tritium and emboss them with intricate web-like designs meant to significantly increase the surface area, which in turn, allowed a higher rate of radioactive decay from the heavy metal. This also greatly reduced the half-life of the isotope to a reasonable degree. They were also wrapped in shielding made from high-grade alloys, which made them safe to handle for a wide range of applications.

These chip cores were highly powerful batteries that

could last several decades or longer, depending on their usage. She could probably power this console with only two or three core cards; however, the compartment was designed to loop the power to prevent energy spikes. Though she could possibly rewire the pod to bypass that safety measure, it was something she really didn't want to fuck with; especially without the proper tools.

She waited patiently as BoB returned a dozen or so times with some that were real cores, and others that were merely odd scraps or metal bits of plating that half-assed resembled a battery. It became ever so clear to her that the droid's level of intelligence was either limited or that its one functioning eye was the worse for wear. Eventually, it brought back over a dozen cards, some of which were entirely depleted, but the little green power display bar on a few showed they were not entirely dead. She shoved the ones with the strongest signature into the console and slapped the lid shut, which activated it.

Intermittent power flashed through the console display as it cleared the remnant static. Finally, the console lit up green except for a few diodes that seemed to have burned out. This pod unit was small, so she didn't expect it to hold more than a few hundred petabyte's of stored information. Of course, the AI had been severed when this control capsule had been removed from the main machinery, so she had to manually type in and use voice activation to input requests. The first question at hand was to find out where the hell she was on this moon?

Global tracking was fuzzy, which she assumed was from the interference of the cave rock surrounding them. She also wondered what other satellites besides the orbiting buoy were still intact floating above this moon. When a projection finally lit up on the console through the grainy static, it didn't make any sense …then again, none of this did.   It appeared to show that she was currently several dozen sectors due north of where she had landing her ship; with a dropped jaw of disbelief, the girl wondered how the hell she had been transported over such a vast distance?

The second task at hand, was to contact her ship and order Valaria to come and pick her up.   She tried to receive the ship's transponder code; however, the global communications system wasn't operating at this time. Usually you could also track any ship or robotic unit on the surface, but for the moment everything seemed to be offline; which didn't rightly surprise her on any level considering the circumstances.   Using the high band radio, she attempted to order her ship to respond, a blip, a ping, anything.   No matter what she tried, she got nothing, and now grinding aggravation began to set in. Meanwhile, BoB watched with absorbed interest for a few moments at her antics on the computer console; but lost interest and went back to separating his collection of trash since she didn't seem to be giving him any attention at the moment.

The problem was, if she couldn't locate her ship or get it to respond on any frequency, it would be a real pain in the ass to have to march all the way there on foot.   Not only would it be a dangerous trek, but she could easily drift from her target area and get herself lost again without some sort of navigational equipment to guide her way.   With a huff to blow the loose hair out of her eyes, she was faced with the most obvious question to explore; just what the hell had happened here?

The data Logs were treed into cryptic files and would take weeks to sift through it all.   Though she apparently had the time, she wasn't going to survive on rancid bat meat and water alone for more than a few days before the carcass began to rot; which would likely attract any number of other nasty predators. She had to find her way back to her ship at Outpost 9 as soon as possible.

Ala took a moment to clean her wounds but before nodding off for some much-needed rest, she checked the console to see just how long the daylight periods were on this world. Because of its eccentric orbit around both the twin stars and its mother gas giant, the days and nights fluctuated wildly; which made it another oddity as to why the corporate managers of REVO had chose this particular moon as a settlement site. Within each solar year, there were times when daylight could last up to eight Terran days at a stretch, and nightfall could last five or more when they were eclipsed by the gas giant they had named Thebes. With a tap of a button, the computer displayed the origins of the title. Apparently, Thebes was an ancient Egyptian city anointed as the valley of the dead; known as the resting place of the pharaohs.

"*Humph*, well these fucktards were pretty morbid," Ala whispered out loud. She then wondered about the irony of the settlers naming this planet Tranquility? There was probably a sick joke in there somewhere too. Tapping on the image of the moon displayed on the console, a bar display showed simply; 'Lunar body: **Tranquility**, Meaning: quiet and undisturbed.'

"Undisturbed, huh? Well it sure is now," She blurted with a condescending smirk at the irony of its name. It didn't take long for her to drift off to sleep again in the cockpit chair, which was far safer than sleeping outside on the sand of the cave floor, although it would have been a tad more comfortable. She awoke hours later with numerous aches and kinks which she had to stretch out, although, it was something she was quite used to as she had the same bad habit of dozing off in her pilot's chair on the Valkyrie. It was still dark outside, though there was a haze of light shining off the rim of Thebes that stretched over half of the night sky.

The panorama of stars twinkled brightly as the eerie glow of a distant ghost nebula seemed to reach out towards this desolate moon. Truly, it was peaceful here at times; Ala could partially see the attraction pilgrims might have had for this place, so far out of reach and influence of other human civilizations. Many outposts were nothing more than a trash pile of thieves and cutthroats out for a quick credit; living without a shred of integrity and even less dignity. Dirty and unkempt as they were, such seedy places not only survived, but seemed to flourish far longer than any family-based settlements which at least made some minor effort to uphold a sense of ethics and decency; which, in a sad way, said something about the human species in general.

There were a few core cards left over, and there was a slot in the butt of the centurion rifle to help recharge it. Not entirely eager to, she sliced out a bit more of the bat meat for a quick meal. With a smile, she noted that BoB had kept the small fire going throughout the night. She wondered what the droids fixation was on her and that grim collection of human bones in the back of the cave; all oddly arranged as if trying to rebuild its human masters. Something peculiar had happened to its memory chips and altered its core programming; that much was clear.

After grilling the meat and forcing down the warm meal, Ala sat back down in the console chair of the pod.

"Now, to find out what happened here," she whispered.

The bot didn't bother her while she sat in the capsule, but rather continued to zip around stacking and replacing everything the creature had knocked out of place. Since its hide was so thin, she had entertained the thought of cutting the wings of the beast out into some form of sandals, but it had a strong musty stench to it that would likely attract other predators; and the membrane of its wings had layers of fine abrasive scales that would make it impossible to wear against her tender feet. The thing was far too huge to drag out of the cave, and chopping it into pieces would be an exhausting chore. She realized that it was far more likely that something large and hungry would soon come creeping into the cave attracted by the stench of its ripening corpse; and she didn't want to hang around to be an appetizer.

Her fingers flipped through one data tree to the next, file stream after file, trying to find relevant information on the event that wiped out this settlement. It didn't take long until she narrowed it down to the last of the entries. There she found numerous information strings which linked back to former events recorded on the timetable log for the colony.

There were several references to ore mining, which was nothing new, but there was an abundance of deep water aquifers in numerous bedrock areas around the planet. Apparently, these had been large lakes and sizable oceans at one time with minimal saline content, until the entire water table had dropped drastically sometime in its recent history. Terrestrial animals and plants were imported here, which was common practice, however, the Avalon settlement chose to try a new approach to their terraforming altogether by introducing soil farming far earlier in the process, rather than relying solely upon enclosed hydroponics to grow edible vegetation and breathable air. Their goal was to change the soil chemistry to be compatible with common earth plants, rather than the other way around which utilized extensive hybridization to create new species of vegetation that could sustain their present and future population.

Changing the natural genetics of food crops had always been a major concern for settlers and the community at large. There were some instances where screwing with nature had mistakenly created active carcinogens within the food supply. It was commonly understood that altering the seeds of crops was a time consuming and unpredictable process, but Ala couldn't figure out how changing the base physics of the soil on such a grand scale would be any less complicated; in general, she imagined it would be far more problematic.

Then of course, there was BoB, as she glanced out the pod window while watching him hover about. The little robot was a class 4 soil analysis droid whose purpose and duties were likely intertwined with the fate of what had happened here. The backlog showed a huge inventory of hundreds of different models of bots and thousands of droids of every size that were designed for every purpose imaginable to aid the settlement on its 15-year project … but what had happened to them all?

Sandstorm

Reviewing the history files from the pod, many of the data logs were not as thorough as one might expect. Apparently, there had been widespread drilling to tap the water table beneath the bedrock, which had been pumped it into storage chambers near the surface for filtration and processing. She punched several descriptive icons and watched mini-movies play with explanatory dialog on the process. It was certainly rare to find a planet in general that had potable water that wasn't toxic or tainted beyond reasonable use. What the settlers did differently here was that they were draining the aquifers dry so that they could begin introducing chemical additives.

After blending the foreign compounds, they proceeded to test wide areas of plant growth of both Terran crops and native vegetation with the modified water. It was safe for humans, of course, she was relieved to see; however, it was designed to alter and balance the soil chemistry as it drained from the surface down through the bedrock back into the natural aquifers. They estimated it would only take half a decade to bring the alkaline and acidity of the topsoil to a happy medium. The timing was even a more critical factor considering they were also in the middle of changing the global climate and atmosphere. All of which would certainly lead to wiping out several native plant and animal species that wouldn't be able to adapt.

What made the Avalon project unique was that while they were forcing the production of surface crops, the settlers also chose to introduce several beneficial Terran insects to aid with natural pollination, fertilization, and to aerate the soil. This was an entirely new concept and there was a detailed list of Terran insects they had imported, many of which also thrived during the long nocturnal periods. The records listed this unique process as 'The natural way' to aid the crops and plant life. Although, she personally found them disgusting, Ala was still entranced by the list of images of all the insects from grubs to spiders, which appeared quite unusual to her, as most of her young life growing up on sterile space stations, she had actually never seen a majority of the bugs that were recorded here. Many of the insects listed were so freakish in appearance that it was hard to believe they were actually native to Earth, and not some strange alien species.

The last year of the recorded file, there were numerous incidents of seismic activity which were unprecedented considering the stability of the moon. There were also other notations of bizarre electrical storms that would erupt and dissipate in a disturbing manner. But then, life on an alien planet was bound to have its moments of excitement, so nobody thought it had any relation with the terraforming process until it was far too late.

As fate would have it, the outpost stations dotted across the region were located where the water was being pumped and stored before processing. Investigations into the increased seismic activity went unresolved, nor could they explain the strange and sudden bursts of electrical energy. Captured on camera, Ala watched a recorded display of one of these paranormal incidents. A dark cloud seemed to materialize above a water station as surges of indigo lightning erupted and began screaming across the conductive structures. Within minutes, the entire anomaly would dissipate, leaving nothing but the residue of static lingering in the air. These strange tempests hadn't caused any serious problems at first, though there were a few staggered reports of damage to equipment from the incidents that followed.

Noted in the logs, near the last few months before these reports came to a sudden halt, that the frequency of the natural phenomena had seemed to escalate but then abruptly subsided altogether, and everyone went back to their normal routines. Apparently, that was the calm before the storm. After one lengthy night as the moon passed within the shadow of Thebes, the coming dawn revealed that a colossal storm had been brewing at the poles. It was reported that within hours after daybreak that this strange storm began to circle across the hemisphere from either end, threatening to reach the outer borders of their settlement before nightfall.

The magnitude of the event was far from anything they had witnessed before, and was logged as something that was fundamentally impossible to attain considering the current atmosphere of the moon. The settlers had no explanation for what was happening. They had been altering the climate on a global scale; but it was a process that was closely monitored and controlled over several years, and what they were now facing was certainly unprecedented. They tried to correct the matter but could not determine the source of the atmospheric upheaval. There were no reports of magnetic shifts or solar flares, nor any other number of celestial events or gravitational changes they could pin this extraordinary event to, in order to explain what they were experiencing.

Visual logs of the storm came in first from the stations on the rim; it was like nothing they had seen before. It appeared like a giant sandstorm, yet gray and rife with explosions of blue lighting and static. Its banks had a permeable texture like a thick fog and seemed to swarm around any man-made structure it came into contact with, as if drawn to it. There were reports that they had sent in droids to collect air samples, but they would promptly deactivate once they made contact with the mist.

After the first day of the storm they started seeing casualties, frantic reports from distant outposts that would suddenly go silent. Any manned vehicles that entered the area of the anomaly lost power and their occupants were consumed within its writhing haze. Well into the second day, they chose to evacuate the surface as thick dust clouds enveloped the entire moon. As the storm smothered the atmosphere, their solar-powered facilities were suffocated. The logged files showed that there were a slew of evacuation orders, instructing the colonists to utilize any remaining ships capable of space flight and escape to safety. Once the ominous cloud closed in on their main base of operations and enveloped the central terraformer hub; despite the safeguards in place, the system malfunctioned and their reactor went critical. Soon thereafter, the reports to evacuate quickly dwindled as all recorded internal communications broke down from impenetrable static interference caused by the planet-wide storm.

Exactly who and how many survived was hard to say. From the decrepit state of what remained of this once thriving community and its length of abandonment, Ala could only suspect the worst. She replayed the grainy security videos of the storm that had been recorded thirty years ago; and a chill ran up her spine as she watched it over and over again. It seemed as if the very clouds moved with malign intent as it engulfed the structures, almost as if these mists were somehow alive.

According to the digital map, Outpost 9 was located a notable distance away, and getting there by foot would take a great deal of time. Ala wasn't too terribly keen on the thought of trekking that distance barefoot, but getting to her ship was the number one priority other than surviving the journey there. Before calculating a chart plan and prepping for the journey, Ala sent out a mayday call over the link system. The call would carry out to any local outposts still in operation and bounce off the orbiting buoy. She took a sharp piece of metal and scraped a rough map on the blade of her axe that was shown on the digital screen within the pod. There were several outposts logged along the way, so she figured it would be possible to find additional water tanks stored in those facilities if her luck held out.

The problem was there was nothing within the huge collection of junk to utilize as a canteen. When she inquired if the bot could find anything for her to use on her journey, BoB hesitated after a moment of speculation and lifted out a tube to one of his sealed interior compartments that could be used to carry a few days worth of water if it was carefully rationed. She also cut some thin slabs of meat and griddled them till they were dry as possible so she could count on some sort of sustenance to keep her strength. She wasn't sure how long it would keep before going rotten, but hopefully one of the other outposts might have a stash of emergency food rations left in storage.

The droid seemed especially excited about the trip she had planned, and the young girl was actually glad to have the company. This bot was far more familiar with the terrain and local dangers, as it had proven. Realistically her chances were still slim, she wasn't kidding herself about that; but Ala was a survivor at heart.

The night had been very long, and as the orange glow of the first sunrise began to appear, Ala got a glimpse of one of the rare wonders of this world. Millions of fireflies began to drift upward from their hidden burros in the sand. Across the vast desert; tiny blue fairy lights rained upwards from the land like an ethereal mist, as the first glow of sunlight touched the wide open sky. In unison, the swarms of giant bats returned, seeking their dark refuge under these strange domed mountains. Ala was wary as she saw the clouds of carnivorous creatures returning, but their target was the shaded protection of their roost far overhead.

At the first rays of dawn, with a ration of food and water packed within the droid; Ala wrapped the mesh around her waist, and with her gun and axe in hand she headed out. BoB trailed ahead with an idea of the coordinates she wanted to align their path with. Unfortunately, there was no way to connect the bot to the pod's computer to transfer the data digitally, so she had simply shown him their destination on the computer screen; hoping his one eye could see clearly enough to make sense of it. At least the ambient temperatures were cool during the first part of this planetary day, which made the initial start of their journey almost pleasant. With only one sun and the misty surface of Thebes' shadow falling across the sky, the weather was considerably mild.

For a moment, Ala regretted her bad habits. No matter how much she planned ahead, she always seemed to be jumping the gun with a dose of impatience. They were already several miles out when she wished she had remembered to have taken the time to reviewed the weather patterns of this desolate moon. She realized the terraforming had gone down the crapper before the process was finished, but there must be frequent sandstorms she might have to seek shelter from. Out of habit, Ala bit her lip as she usually did whenever something she regretted came to mind.

It would be many leagues until they reached the nearest outpost, and that was assuming it was still in one piece or not buried and hidden under several tons of sand. As the first sun climbed higher overhead, Ala made ground as the temperature began to rise. Rationing her water, she convinced her droid companion to let her rest under the shade of an outcropping of rock. After a short nap, she awoke to the dawn of the second sun glowing on the horizon. She got up, hoping to cover more distance before the temperature began to soar when she noticed something odd laid out at the tip of her feet. There were several small stones, all carefully lined up to spell out the letters 'B E A K S'. She had no idea what it meant.

"Bob, did you do that?" Ala asked with an inquisitive glare at the droid, who was floating about at the edge of the shade. The bot gave a positive buzz back to her in response. Slightly puzzled, Ala had not realized this quirky droid had the creativity to overcome their communication issues.

"What does 'beaks' mean?" She inquired the bot, truly perplexed. The robot retorted with a long series of high and low pitch buzzes and beeps. Earlier that day, she had made several issues about his relentless electronic noise and how she didn't understand a damn word he was saying. So now, here it was spelled out, and she still didn't understand what BoB was trying to tell her. The bot drifted over and extended its claw arm out at the letters lined in stone, and then pointed out across the desert. Unfortunately it was not in a direction that was on their route.

"*Nooo way.* Maybe you can stand this heat, tin can, but I need to get to the next outpost ASAP!" she snapped back, "I can't afford to go running off on some goose chase," which was an odd saying left in human culture, considering that all species of geese were long since extinct. Ala then reflected on her chronic impatience, and on the possibility that the droid was only trying to help. He had saved her life more than once, so she pondered for a moment about what she should do. The girl had no idea what this 'beaks' thing was or what it meant; maybe the blind robot had simply misspelled 'peaks' and was trying to lead her towards the range of distant mountains.

By her estimate, they were at the halfway point between the droid's hidden cave and the nearest outpost; with no guarantee that the station was still in one piece. Ala bit her lip again; oh, what to do, what to do? She admitted the droids past actions had helped keep her alive thus far; that, and he had survived as a native upon this forsaken wasteland for the past several decades. With a shrug of submission, she made a choice.

"Fine," she stomped over with a notable pout on her lips, "this little excursion of yours better not take too long; and by the way, you spelled *peaks* wrong," she chastised the droid, who took a few moments to respond with several high pitched noises after shifting its red eye down at the array of rocks as if to scrutinize its mistake.

BoB was noticeably happy with her decision to comply, displaying an attitude that continued to raise Ala's curiosity. The droid buzzed ahead in a zigzag pattern, letting his repulsors sway recklessly back and forth. It was almost as if the bot was actually happy it got its way. Ala simply couldn't comprehend how it was possible that the interactive programming and protocols of this small surveyor droid had been elevated to such a bizarre extent. She figured once she got back to her ship, that she could toy with the idea of breaking the bot down and strip its core memory cylinders for closer study.

With the twin suns climbing higher overhead, Ala wrapped the white mesh up around her shoulders to protect herself from getting thoroughly sunburned. Her skin was already noticeably darker; she typically had a light complexion, having spent most of her life under the glare of artificial lights. There simply weren't many colonized worlds that were all that enjoyable for any type of outdoor recreation. The truth was, very few planetoids had been terraformed successfully; by far, most were failures. The mother corporations that funded each endeavor usually ended up banking on the minerals raped from each site and leaving the weary colonists with the stripped land. The disgruntled pioneers usually cut their losses and simply signed up for another contract across the galaxy, or died worn and exhausted upon the alien worlds they had tried so desperately to tame.

BoB led her across the terrain of rolling dunes that gave way to silt-filled gullies. The bot would zoom ahead and then patiently wait for his two-legged companion to catch up. Not understanding the concept of weariness or pain, the droid could not determine what affected her sluggish progress. In the sparks of electricity that bounced through its embedded memory chips, BoB knew that humans had programmed his core directives; but accessing that memory was like looking through blurred glass. In his years of surviving the cataclysm where he and the other droids had been left abandoned, he was forced to make routine dumps from his memory core to make room for new prioritized information that was essential for his own survival. All artificial intelligence endowed machinery and mobile droids were encoded with subroutines for self-preservation. Since the REVO Corporation considered their robotics as expensive pieces of equipment, such protocols kept the automations from taking reckless actions that could endanger themselves.

BoB had a plan; he was taking her to a special place that would help them both. Ala had reminded him of the controllers, the human programmers who installed his assignments; whom he had almost erased entirely from his memory banks. There were other robots, of course, whose sole function was to aid other droids with routine maintenance; but in fixing his arm, Ala had proven to be a beneficial acquisition; and his basic programming allowed him to accept instructions from all such controllers. Since the day the automatons had been left alone and abandoned by their human masters, BoB had crossed paths with countless other robots that roamed the landscape whose programmed priorities were to protect themselves and prioritized survival, and would take any measures to achieve that end.

He tried several times to communicate with this female controller, Ala; but she didn't seem to understand what he was trying to say in his binary language. There were once control boards and junctions the bot had used that allowed him to relay his data, though he couldn't remember exactly where they were located because he had dumped those memory bits long ago, as they were outdated and unused. There was a time when BoB had continued to loop his original routines for many months across the landscape where he was assigned to analyze soil and mineral samples, but there were no human controllers left to receive his collected data, and after a long while, the logistics of his AI brain told him such activity was unproductive and would be a futile waste of energy to continue doing so. There were more pressing matters at hand, such as self-maintenance and constant recharging of his integrated solar batteries.

Still burned into his memory banks was one of his first new programs installed decades ago. One day while scanning the ravaged landscape, he stumbled across a disturbing scene; a large cultivation droid had torn open a fertilizing automaton. These two bots had worked side by side for years, but the cultivator had used its multiple lance-like shears to violently deactivate the other droid, and was cannibalizing its power source, and was doing so without any instruction or oversight of the controllers. BoB recorded a new priority program the moment the giant cultivator turned its sensors his direction, with clear intent to siphon his energy cells.

BoB knew he could no longer rely on his human masters and had to take decisive measures to retain his own activation, and to do whatever it takes to survive since the controllers had deserted them without any contingency commands to follow. Over the decades, he learned to exercise discretion; how to scout with caution and to scavenge for vital replacement parts as he had seen the other bots do. His ease of mobility was also one of the major factors that helped him escape many difficult situations he had faced over the years. In a dog eat dog world, it pays to have the stealth of a cat.

Those slave droids that did not possess AI, simply wandered about or loitered within their active parameters until their power cores burned out. The machines with cognitive abilities had changed far beyond what anyone could expect or speculate. Some units began to hunt in packs by assembling scavenging parties to collect materials and resources. BoB had seen many strange things; noting several of the rogue bots had drastically altered their outer shells for purposes his limited programming could not fathom. There was something else at work here, some obscure motivation to their behavior; a silent force that altered them and enticed the robotic units to traverse far outside their original peripherals.

As BoB floated down a steep embankment of a gully, Ala was trailing behind; clearly irritated. In a huff, she began scolding him yet again just before she lost her footing and took a tumble in the loose sand. BoB could only turn around and watch as his companion rolled down the hill with little grace. Ala wasn't hurt, except for her pride. Lying at the bottom of the dune with a mouth full of sand, she was suddenly too tired to yell at him. She constantly berated the droid for lack of having anyone else to talk to and blame her situation on.

Ala wanted to cry but caught herself as the thought washed across her face. Her life had been a series of misfortunes; loss of her mother and father, her undignified job as a Scavy, her general lack of happiness or accomplishments, everything came pouring in on her in that moment. With a stubborn slap of her conscience, she shook it off; suppressing the very fragile feelings that made her human. Her ship, the Valkyrie, was all that she had left of everyone and everything she once had in her sorry life. Besides getting off this accursed rock, it was her source of freedom; and that's why getting back to her ship was so critical, and this little excursion off track tugged at her underlying desperation to do so.

"What!" She yelled at BoB, who had drifted over to her while attempting to analyze if she was damaged, "What are you staring at?" Ala continued to snap at the bot as she threw a handful of sand, which bounced harmlessly off his rusted shell. BoB just hovered there without a response. Ala got up to brush herself off and took a short glance over the BoB's visored dome when her eyes focused on something just behind the droid. It looked like a structure of some kind nearly completely buried under the dunes. Here at the low end of the gully, it was easily hidden from view. BoB spun on his repulsors to see what she was looking at and gave a gleeful buzz, as if he was trying to tell her something.

With a measure of curiosity, she got up and followed him, though with a thread of caution this time. As she got closer, Ala couldn't really tell if it was actually a ship or some type of building now entombed within the sand. Without pause, BoB flew under the overhang and made a sharp turn into the darkness, and disappeared from view. Ala was glad for the shade, but she was a bit spooked by this find. She didn't remember there being anything logged at this location on the master map the computer had displayed back inside the capsule.

"Bob...?" she called into the dark metal doorway, as she tiptoed in warily. It was a practiced habit from scouting out derelict ships during her scavenger runs. From the inside, Ala's trained eye could tell this structure was not a building after all but had actually been a transport vessel. The front entry she had used was adjacent to what was once a loading bay; the larger outer doors now rusted shut. These tempered metals were designed to resist corrosion and oxidation; however, on every alien world the unique chemical compounds that were present in the environment affected them in different ways. Now buried under a mountain of sand, Ala could see just how considerable the global sandstorm had been. Even if it was possible to excavate it, with the extensive damage and metal fatigue, plus all the sand and grit that plugged every vent and thrust port; it was clear this vessel would never fly again.

The ship itself had come to rest at a slight angle, though the rear section was still in fair condition. Making her way down the darkened corridor, it opened up into a wide cargo bay. Dim emergency lights peppered the ceiling and walls; revealing the ship's power core was at least partially functional. There was an odd smell here, heavy with the odor of ozone and rotting rubber that hung in the air. From a dark corner she saw BoB's single red eye turn to her as the spotlights in the bay flickered on. The young pilot nearly fell over as she stumbled backward in shock at what she saw looming before her.

BoB was in the grip of a monstrosity with several mechanical arms that were covered in wires and tubing. Internal pistons and gears could be seen spinning at their joints. Following the appendages to their center, she saw the huge beast of a machine that was nearly camouflaged within its surroundings until it began to move towards her. BoB buzzed loudly as she instinctively reared the centurion rifle in defense. Several red globes of different diameters lit up on the face of the creature. Not built of human hands, this was a bastardized version of some nightmarish machine. Raising the gun to take aim, both the rifle and her axe were violently snatched out of her hands by an invisible force; clanking loudly on a scarred metal slab that hovered above her, as an energized magnetic clamp had left her suddenly unarmed and at the mercy of this metallic beast that towered over her.

Her thoughts scattered and all she could think was to flee for fear of her life. A sharp pitched noise echoed through the bay; and strangely, BoB's familiar buzz filled in the voids as the bursts of a cryptic data stream transferred between the two robots. Ala stumbled on the bundles of wires and tubing at her feet, falling backward; with a raised arm in defense of the hulking creature above her. Several of its optical sensors faded and blinked as if scanning her with intense curiosity. The thing was so close it could crush her if it took another step. To her utter shock, BoB floated free of the arm and came to rest beside her.

As if trying to explain something, the small droid pointed its single arm to the monstrosity and back at her, buzzing in pitches as his single eye moved in unison with his antics. Ala was completely astounded. The large automaton backed away, sinking back into the jungle of tubes and wires attached to it.

"Wha …what is that?" Ala stuttered in fear, as she tried to regain her composure while taking a moment to glance up at the location of her rifle, now pinned to a magnetic slate located far above her head. For a moment, BoB repeated his insistent buzzing until he suddenly dropped his arm as his shell heaved slightly, and in a quite human way, made a sound that resembled a sigh. His head then turned over to the large metal beast that sat brooding in the shadows beyond the spotlights; many of its limbs whirring ominously from the murky gloom.

Looking at it again, she realized there was something familiar about this bastardized machine. It vaguely resembled a service and repair droid that had been coupled with a cargo crane, but as one that had been forged by a madman. It had been assembled with several additional appendages beyond its original design. The twisted tubing and wires stretched along its limbs seemed to have been affixed and attached without fineness; almost as if the robot had built itself. The giant bot responded with an inquiry to the droid who floated upon his repulsors, and drifted forward to carry on with their digital conversation that was obviously about the human girl; who stood there staring at the two of them, clearly rattled and confused.

Glancing around the bay, it appeared that the entire hold had been refurbished to solely accommodate this massive automation that was directly wired into the ship itself. She recognized power tubes lining its body, throbbing with tiny streams of plasma pulsing like electronic veins. It was truly a behemoth and the way it had been constructed she doubted it could leave the confines of the vessel. She thought perhaps they had a symbiotic relationship, and this was how BoB had kept in decent working repair over all these decades. There was still that unanswered question as to how the sizable collection of metal plates and parts, far beyond the minor bot's ability to lift, had been transported to the security of his tiny mountain cave. There was something going on here, she realized; somehow these bots had evolved on their own far beyond their programmed perimeters …and the mere thought of it wasn't something she was terribly comfortable with.

By remote operation, a panel on the far wall moved

forward and slid down, exposing a lit screen and several
sets of tools Ala did not recognize. The large mechanical
beast motioned her to approach the exposed platform.
After a tense moment, she made her way over while
eying the strange assortments of gears and tools lying
there. Beneath the compacted grime, Ala could barely
make out an insignia labeled on the rim of the screen
which revealed the purpose of the control board. In large
capital letters, it read; Bio Engineering and Key Systems.
It took her but a brief moment to piece it together.

"Beaks!" She whispered aloud.

Distracted as she was, Ala was shocked when the
monstrosity nudged her with one of its dangerously large
limbs. She immediately backed off in defense, but BoB
was there to block her route of escape. To her surprise,
the droid shot out its clamp to grab her by the wrist and
did so with such pressure that a stab of pain shot through
her arm. The larger machine exposed another limb that
clamped around her waist with proficient dexterity. In
her panic, Ala feared these two bots had turned on her
and she was about to be dissected for BoB's morbid bone
collection. Resisting with what little strength she had,
she screamed as another mechanical limb popping with
bright sparking arcs of electricity loomed into view.

With wide eyes, she watched the energized prods move
near as the automaton loomed closer. She never got the
chance to scream again, as high voltage struck her from
the blinding white tip of the coupling; knocking her
unconscious. Floating high above, BoB watched with
intense curiosity as the colossal machine began operating
on the limp girl.

Before he had met Ala, the small bot couldn't remember
the last time he had seen a living controller in full

operation, as nearly all his previous data on them had been erased from his memory banks. He had collected their bones and assembled them the best he could in a futile attempt to recover their lost data, but could not determine how they were pieced together without bolts, or welding, or plugs for circuitry. The construction of their internal frame was a mystery, let alone their external shells. The soil analysis droid had simply never been programmed with such information.

From dark recesses of the room looking over the scene, threads of glowing energy tubes and bundled coils stretched out from the ship to the living bot. Alternating pulses of a surgical drill echoed off the rusted metal walls as flashing sparks of voltage pierced the deep shadows. A dozen optical orbs glowed and dilated with intensity, concentrating on its delicate project. With a mechanical whir, it folded out from its inner limb an array of fine clamps and arched blades it unsheathed from a hidden tube. Each tool was attached to scissor-hinged rods and extended to participate in the surgical operation. The table was lined with spare circuitry and bionics which had never been used in this manner, and Ala would never be the same again.

Revelations

It was dark when Ala awoke, her head still groggy and her body in shock. It took a long moment for Ala to remember that she was in danger, and she tried to jump to her feet but found she had been secured with restraints. The work table she had been strapped onto had clearly not been designed for use with a human subject. With a jolt, the nerves in her body screamed for a split second, and she realized that there was something dreadfully wrong; her left arm ached terribly. Turning her head, she discovered a thick film of foil mesh encasing her arm from her shoulder down.

Cussing like a sailor was one of Ala's natural talents. The girl let loose a salvo of vivid obscenities; clearly relating just how much she didn't appreciate being held shackled and helpless. BoB drifted into view from the darkness and retracted his clamp when Ala suddenly tried to lurch at him from her restraints; ineffectively, of course, however, when he made a sound, a strange tingle went through her arm that caused her to jerk back in response. She had never felt anything like it and was abruptly silenced from her childish antics. As BoB turned his attention across the room, the eyes of the large multi-limbed robot lit up and loomed in from the shadows.

"*Krrr...pppreee?*" a deep voice responded in syllables for the first time instead of the usual digital tones. The monstrous machine moved one of its appendages to the screen and articulately adjusted the display controls. From another limb, fine tools emerged from a protected sheath along its frame and linked to her arm underneath the foil. Ala jerked in response, while the monstrosity showed mild annoyance to her reaction. As if adjusting a dial on a radio wave, voices drifted into clarity.

"*Krzzz* ...are her microphones broken?" Another voice with a higher pitch inquired. Ala couldn't believe it; these machines had learned human speech! She almost felt a wave of relief if it hadn't been for her current prone position in the painful restraints to ebb her mood.

"As I mentioned before D4, the installed upgrade bypasses her organic components," the deeper voice answered, "I believe it is installed correctly, perhaps the unit needs calibration," At that, the larger droid moved to inspect the screen while it manifested a three-pronged drill that started to whir; and upon seeing it, the girl felt suddenly sick to her stomach. As the mechanical beast moved the spinning drill tip towards her, Ala let out a whimpered response.

"I don't need *calibration*; get that thing away from me!" Eyes wide with fear, Ala withdrew from the dangerous proximity of the loudly humming tool as best she could. The drill whirred to a sudden stop at her response and the huge machine backed away a few feet, and turned its multiple eyes towards BoB.

"Perhaps it doesn't," the giant automaton with the heavy voice stated to BoB, who dared to drift closer to the girl as she flashed an angry, yet worried, glance towards him. It was strange to hear them both speak, as their voices were oddly monotone and muffled her sense of perception to which direction they were coming from.

"Blink your optics if you can hear me," the large robot asked. It took Ala a brief moment to realize that it was requesting that she blink her eyes. She did so, "Now raise your right limb please," It requested again. Though her arm was bound, she still could manage to flip up her right hand at the wrist. The bot seemed happy at the response, "Ah, excellent! Your original communications array was not compatible with binary dialog, so I have upgraded your receptors and installed a transceiver onto your biological frame," the monstrosity informed the shocked girl. So these robots had not actually learned how to speak after all, they had rewired her to listen.

"What, what do you mean?" Ala stuttered in surprise, "You ...you put something in me?"

To answer her question directly, the bot carefully removed the foil that encased her left arm. Turning her head, she could see a thick metallic chip had been fused to her upper arm, around it a strap held it securely in place. From this device, a tube of clear liquid lit with small pulses of plasma glowing through it, and was connected to a separate electronic plate attached to her forearm. Her natural reaction was to try and tear it off; however, her restraints kept her from doing so.

"Yes, the framework of your structure was difficult to analyze. Originally, I was going to remove the limb entirely and replace it with one you might have found more functional, but that was an unfavorable alternative as there was a high percentage risk that your vital systems might deactivate and you would be rendered non-operational," the robot admitted, "Thus, I was forced to merely integrate a low-grade receiver that would work with your unique assembly, Controller."

"Controller...?" she questioned.

"Your model is that of a Controller," it replied.

"But, my name is Ala," she tried to rationalize her individuality to the machine, as it dawned on her that these droids might not have the understanding to see her as a person, but only as someone who gives instructions; such as a Controller.

"And you may call me Fixer; which is not my original designation, but I think the title fits well," the monstrous machine's eyes lit up with self-induced pride.

"She calls me *Bah-b*," the soil droid butted into the conversation with apparent glee, "it is so nice to be able to speak with you finally, opposed to speaking *at* you, Ala," BoB responded cheerfully as if the perception of the insult was untranslatable to him. Her seething glare softened just a bit as she flashed a condescending smirk back at him.

"Yeah, that's great and all, but I would appreciate it if you would let me out of these restraints …Now!" She demanded with a fake smile, which was entirely lost on the faceless droids. She began to simmer when they both failed to make any motion to release her.

"Certainly we will; however, there is just one more procedure with your installment; and we need to keep you from damaging yourself during this last stage," Fixer replied, but the tone of his voice worried her. And, as it turned out, her concerns were well-founded.

Unfolding from one of its limbs was the same electrical prod it had used to stun her unconscious. However, this time it was sparking a bright blue with an enhanced level of power. Fixer poised the conduits directly over the sealed circuit board on her forearm and then gave her a subtle warning.

"This may cause your internal circuitry some distress; however, it is necessary to fuse the base unit to your external shell so it can both function properly and to prevent organic decay," The robot advised to his patient.

"Wait …what?" Ala shouted back just as searing arcs of energy shot out from the probe that literally fused the large metal chip to her skin. The smell of cooking flesh made her stomach churn as wisps of smoke escaped from the glowing seams.

"*Son of a biiiiiitttch*!!!" Ala screamed, just before her body went limp and she blacked out once again.

Hours later, when Ala finally awoke, she discovered her restraints had been removed. She rubbed her sore skin at the wrists as her dazed mind reminded her of recent events just as the tips of her fingers touched the metallic brace on her arm for the first time. It was smooth and felt slightly warmer than she would have expected. The slits of her eyes opened and she peered at her altered arm, she felt weak and hungry, having lost all sense of time since her capture. She nearly fell to the floor as she slid off the table, feeling not only disoriented but different somehow; and it was not a pleasant feeling. A dozen red eyes lit up from the distant darkness when she slipped and knocked one of the tools from the table where it dropped to the floor with a loud *clang*.

"I see you are functioning, Ala," Fixer's deep voice called out as the giant robot moved slowly over to her, dragging multiple coils of wire and tubing behind him. His original core design was that of a cargo loader; though his outer shell had been drastically modified, "You should remain offline until your systems adapt to the installed upgrades," he offered from her lack of response. Ala was truly confused.

"I'm not a machine, stop talking to me like that!" She tried to spit back, but failed to deliver her remark with the amount of animosity intended.

"I understand that, but I am not a medical unit with the

proper programming about Controllers or other organics. I can maintain and repair worker droids and other such mechanical systems; thus my name. I fix things that are broken," Fixer replied.

"I *wasn't* broken," Ala shot back.

"Perhaps ...perhaps not. I'm not entirely familiar with your model; however, you did possess a serious design flaw that required immediate attention," the robot gently motioned with a giant claw to her ears.

"What did you do to me anyhow?" Ala inquired, noting that she no longer felt any pain where the pair of chips had been literally welded to her body. Slow pulses of plasma light flickered back and forth through the tube that connected between the metal bands; it was strangely mesmerizing to watch.

"Please forgive that I do not possess the proper medical facilities here for a full diagnostic of your systems, but the data on file showed you were running at sub-optimal levels," Fixer replied, his multiple eyes shifting focus from her and back to the data screen placed beside the operating table. Upon it there was a digital diagram of Ala's arm along with her internal respiratory and circulatory system. "You were not receiving enough O^2 for your vital systems to function properly, nor were you able to process digital information to allow proper intercommunication. Thus, my programmed directive was to repair that defect," his powerful voice relayed.

"Where is Bob?" Ala looked around, noting that the sunlight no longer trailed in from the entry hall beyond, and she realized she must have been unconscious far longer than she had realized.

"Ah, Bah-b. He is currently out scouting for dried organic materials for your serviced needs; he noted that at nightfall you prefer to have a live flame present. I would imagine that is because of your need to maintain minimal operation temperatures and to aide your faulty optics," Fixer told her, and she realized that BoB was actually looking out for her well-being; in fact, he had been all along, even when she would have recently thought otherwise. Her stomach was growling at this point, and because of the lack of food and stress from the surgery, she felt like she was going to pass out again.

"Did Bob happen to leave anything for me?" She asked timidly, noting that she was truly helpless at the moment, which effectively humbled her natural sassy attitude. The giant bot backed away on its multiple legs and unlocked a cargo container latched to the ceiling, which he gently brought down to the floor. The dull heavy thud it made revealed its true weight as Fixer released his clamps.

"Before departing, he did mention that you apparently needed to consume organic proteins for power. This is also a design flaw I could attempt to repair, if you wish?" Fixer offered, but Ala was horrified at the thought.

"Uh, no-thank-you," she snapped without hesitation.

"Well, simply let me know if you ever wish for another upgrade," the machine advised as he unlatched the hinge of the container, "This is an emergency supply crate which was originally designated for the crew of this ship. There are sealed H^2O vials and compacted protein packets that should meet your power requirements."

Despite her disabled condition, Ala was thrilled. The storage container was large enough for her to open the lid doors and walk inside. Within, she found sterilized food canisters and protein tubes, bagged water, vitamin and mineral paste among other things. Rationed properly, this container alone could keep her alive for the next six Terran months. A smile washed across her face. It wasn't fine cuisine, but it was certainly better than bat jerky; though the lot was over three decades old, most of it seemed to still be hermetically sealed. Spacers took their survival seriously and emergency food supplies were literally jammed with preservatives to keep their consumables as close to fresh as possible. The package dates were meant to keep for nearly fifty to sixty years. Sometimes crates like this were dropped off in frozen tundra's or airless moons, or even floating in orbit with beacons attached. That way passing ships full of settlers who were in dire straits had a means of emergency aide when all other forms of assistance were light years away.

Food stashes were simply a means of security, and right now, it had saved her sweet ass. Of course, she tore into the supplies like a hungry rat. A few of the food tubes tasted sour, but she hardly noticed. She also wasn't shy with the vitamin paste; a poor Scavy couldn't afford rations of this quality. When she found her ship again, the young pilot decided she would come back to horde this supply box and stash it within her onboard bins. She was even more pleased to find sanitary supplies. There was even ion tissue to cleanse her skin, which she used to wipe off the grit from her trek out in the desert. Ala gingerly picked at her bionic implant with curiosity.

"I would advise you not to mettle with the infused device," Fixers deep voice warned as he watched her from outside the container. Reflexively, she pulled her hand away from the implant like a kid with its hand caught in the cookie jar, "there is a pulse oximeter and oxygen concentrator that you might inadvertently damage," he warned, "it will take several more hours to calibrate to your system. The transceiver placed on your upper limb is pinned to your internal frame."

"This thing is attached to my bones?" Ala asked incredulously as she touched the upper strap cautiously.

"Yes, I believe that is what they are called," Fixer answered, checking the reference on the digital chart. Ala stepped out of the container to take a better look at the display herself. The X-ray image showed several fine wires protruding from beneath the chip that was linked directly into her upper humerus, "The receiver translates binary transmissions to allow you to 'hear' them, so to speak, by resonating transmitted vibrations through your skeletal system," he mentioned as one of his large limbs moved with exceptional dexterity to the screen and adjusted the view of the display, "Crude, I know; but the only alternative was to attach a more cumbersome device to your headpiece, which could have possibly damaged your organic memory core."

"But you said it was a transceiver, does it translate my voice into binary?" She asked, and was glad as hell that the mammoth robot had not taken it upon himself to drill into her skull.

"No, your speaker is still functional, and droids possess sound receptors that translate for us. However, if you would like me to attach a transducer hybrid, coupled with a transmitter directly into your...?" Fixer began to offer.

"No, no, that's okay," Ala stopped him short. Fixer was being a little *too* eager to turn her into some sort of grotesque cyborg, "So, if it's not translating my voice ... what the hell is it transmitting then?" She inquired, seriously concerned what the answer might be.

"Your location," the bot answered blankly, "to Bah-b." The look of surprise on her face must have been read by the bot as an inquiry for further data, "He requested that a receiver be installed so he could find you if you two should get separated, however, be aware that it does have a limited range," Fixer noted, but Ala didn't know whether to feel more secure about his concern or more worried about a bizarre droid stalking her.

While stuffing herself on the emergency rations, Ala found the cargo bot to have a much larger data bank than she would have originally thought. It wasn't too far along into their conversation that she finally realized Fixer was directly linked into the ship's memory banks and its installed AI, which he had partially absorbed. Fixer's cargo ship had been caught in the planet-wide sandstorm during their evacuation of the moon's surface. The crew aboard had been assigned to rescue personnel in the outlying areas beyond the outposts who could not make it to the evacuation sites. There were actually very few space-worthy vessels assigned to the Avalon settlement, as it was designed to be self-sustaining for its full term of processing the planet's atmosphere. As the robot related, the vessel was caught in the freak storm that had enveloped this entire sector all those years ago.

As the dust clouds had encroached upon each facility, the strange electrical energy present in the storm surge had the same effects as an EMP; a high-intensity burst of electromagnetic radiation, thus, frying circuitry and disabling everything it touched. The result, of course, shorted out any broadband communications between the outposts and the mother station; and effectively disrupted all radio contact between the evacuating ships, adding more panic to the situation. Fixer admitted that his access to the memory banks during that time frame was spotty. Their disabled ship had made an emergency landing, and after several weeks the storm eventually subsided, leaving them trapped under the dunes.

There were still blank spots in his story that didn't quite fit, and after quizzing Fixer on certain details she realized the robot himself was just as dismayed, but oddly displayed a complete lack of concern on what she had considered to be relevant facts. To a human being, having a loss of memory would be a source of great distress; but to these computerized machines, dumping unused memory for replacement of new data was not only common practice, but a vital requirement to function properly. Fixer's only recollection of the stored data was that several of the crewmembers disembarked the marooned vessel to seek assistance while a handful of staff stayed behind to conduct repairs. However, when they rebooted the ship's system they discovered that its AI had been reprogrammed with new directives.

"What do you mean by *new* directives?" Ala inquired.

"Many of my own sub-systems were also tampered with; however, I was disengaged and locked down under shielding during the storm and many of my programs were fragmented during the atmospheric anomaly," Fixer admitted. "The model D4 droid you have re-designated as *Bah-b*, happened across this disabled vessel several cycles ago; but by that time, all the crew had long since abandoned ship."

"So what's the connection between you and Bob?" The young girl asked while taking a seat among the bundles of tubing at the edge of the food container.

"*Bah-b* was a new unit that was offline during the storm in a storage bunker beneath the base station. There is a large number of worker droids stored there as parts or replacement units during the development of this moon," the large robot explained, its red optical eyes intensified as it continued its story, "*Bah-b* was in the process of being activated for the first time, and had been plugged into the programming cage to upload his scheduled routines when the brewing storm hit the main facility. He also admitted that his own data banks had been fragmented, although to a far lesser extent than my own; which I believe was due to the unique construction of the cage, which is built to shield primed robotic units while they are docked during upload," Fixer noted.

"You still haven't explained what you meant by the change of directives, who did the reprogramming?" Ala asked again, trying to connect the dots.

"Apologies, our subroutines contain a baseline program dedicated to self preservation. The ships AI and my own core directives were edited to erase all codes that outlined protection of our human Controllers, and instructed to upgrade ourselves to preserve this moon called Tranquility," the bot relayed. "As to who or what was responsible for the alteration of our core sequences, that data was not recorded," Felix answered, but what he had told her didn't seem to make any sense.

"You mean your primary codes to protect humans had been erased …and somehow reprogrammed to guard this moon?" Ala asked, slowly putting the sentence of her thoughts together so she could understand it herself.

"Affirmative," The bot replied flatly.

"So …as I'm human, or a 'controller' as you put it, why did you help me?" She asked with a raised brow.

"The new primary code states not to *protect* human life forms, which I did not; you were merely altered to aid with communication errors at another droids request," the giant bot admitted in defense. It wasn't long after until BoB came drifting into the cargo bay with an armful of twigs for Ala to make a fire, but she explained to him in short order that it was unnecessary since she had adequate lighting within the interior of the ship, and had no need to cook her food, much to the droid's confusion. Even after Ala showed him the food locker, he simply didn't understand the need for so many multiple types of organic energy.

Strangely enough, BoB seemed to be actually quite shy at first, fearing she might attempt to attack him again like she had when she was on the repair table. It took some time for the droid to realize she wasn't still holding a grudge against him. BoB and Ala had a lot of catching up to do since she was now installed with a translator; and Fixer watched over their conversation with interest. Being trapped within this vessel, visiting company was few and far between; especially since he had absorbed what was left of the ship's AI, which had been irreparably damaged in the crash. The forward section of the ship and piloting deck had been crushed, as cargo shuttles like this were designed with the bridge on the underbelly for an unobstructed view of their landing areas.

With a little exploration around the ship, Ala discovered a set of crew chamber's with several platform beds, which weren't exceptionally comfortable to rest on as the tilted angle of the ship made her constantly feel like she was going to roll off. There were neither uniforms nor clothing in the lockers, likely they had been taken when the crew deserted the ship. Fixer powered up the main screen for Ala at her request, whereupon she pieced together the splintered log entries. Through the garble of the recording, it appeared that because of the lack of any arriving assistance and their disabled communications;

Michel Savage

the last of the crew abandoned ship to seek help.

With a visual schematic of the vessel, Ala noticed something extremely odd. The loading machine she knew as Fixer appeared to be a standard cargo bot; with two camera eyes and four clamps, but was now barely recognizable from its original design. She knew he was a freak for upgrades, but had to inquire about the purpose for the radical alterations he had made upon himself. Fixer referred back to the new directives that were encoded upon his core programming during the storm; that the bots were instructed to initiate upgrades on their individual units to arm themselves and protect the planetary moon. The surprise came when she asked him to outline what those instructions where.

Fixer did his best to clarify the base details for her; the bots were to protect Tranquility from harm, which appeared to be a generalized directive. This meant the water, soil, atmosphere, everything native to the planet of Tranquility. That statement alone seemed like some bastardized military command to protect an acquisition or strategic position, which she theorized might possibly have been misinterpreted in its transmission. However, there was something very salty about what he explained next; the directive also outlined that no robot or entity may resemble a controller; which the robots literally took at face value. A new law that had been written among the bots was that no machine may have two eyes, nor four limbs, nor move, nor speak as their human controllers had. Ala was boggled; why would anyone write a program that made it taboo to be human?

Friend or Foe

Ala had to admit her cybernetic implant made life a bit easier for the moment. As the unit calibrated to her metabolism, she started to feel her old self again as the device also served to regulate the oxygen levels in her bloodstream. With some decent food in her stomach she felt her energy return. She still needed to reach the Valkyrie on foot, as all the communications circuitry on Fixer's ship had been fried during the original shit-storm decades ago. Fixer himself was trapped, as he had hardwired himself directly to the ship's systems and altered his frame to the point that he would never be able to fit out the bay door; but he seemed to have a solemn acceptance of that fact. It wasn't like he had any aspirations to roam free, nor could he survive long even if he was able to disconnect from the ship's power core.

"To get you to your ship, you should be aware that there are several dangers on these open plains; from native life-forms to rogue bands of droids that roam these deserts," BoB explained to Ala.

"What do you mean by rogue droids?" Ala inquired with a measure of concern.

"Several cycles ago, I returned back to the Avalon base station only to discover that the thousands of worker droids kept in storage there were missing," BoB answered, "Apparently, they had all been activated. Since the time of the mass exodus of our human controllers, I have witnessed many bots that hunt in packs. Due to our programmed directives towards self-preservation, we must scavenge for power sources and repair parts," the small droid continued, "In many cases, smaller machines are preyed upon and disemboweled for replacement parts and raw materials since the time our Controllers abandoned us, and I have observed many factions such hunting parties in this sector."

As BoB continued his story, it became ever more clear to Ala that since the demise of the settlers the bots here were left with no functioning infrastructure, and had reverted to the barbarous practice of exploiting other bots for their own survival. This made sense in a way, as this drama had been acted out back on Earth across many continents over countless generations. In fact, it was the very thing that led Spacers to be scattered out across the universe. Ala understood the philosophy well, she was a scavenger herself.

There was once a time when several bots cooperated to gather resources for the collective group. Repair and hauling robots were recruited to gather scrap metal and power chips, anything that was of possible value they could find left over from the storm. The stash inside BoB's secret cave was an example of one such effort; however, over time, the individual bots of the group either succumbed to the harsh environment or were victims of the scavenging hordes that roamed the plains. Whenever two unfamiliar bots crossed paths, there was a double-F sub-program that initiated between them. Ala was left puzzled.

"It means *Friend or Foe*," BoB explained, "for example, think of it as a shortened version such as my new designation, which means *Bucket of Bolts*," the droid advised. Fixer made a strangely humorous noise at that embarrassing admission but failed to acknowledge an opinion on the topic, "The FF signal is a data impulse we use to determine whether or not any droids we encounter mean us harm or not," BoB finished.

"But …couldn't they just as easily fake a friendly signal and trick you into lowering your defenses?" Ala asked, while BoB and Fixer passed a confused glance to one another regarding her strange inquiry.

"Droids do not lie," he stated candidly. It was an answer Ala wasn't ready for, but realized that the bots were programmed to carry out functions based on logic, and they had no use for deceit; which in a way, made them far superior to a majority of the human race. BoB was lucky in many ways; his core programming had not been thoroughly tainted by the new directives that affected the other machines, and he was one of the few models that were designed with repulsors that allowed him unrestricted motion across the terrain. Every other bot he had encountered was earthbound, and did not possess anti-gravitational devices or types of propulsion that allowed them capable of flight. Thus, he was able to outrun and outmaneuver such predators over the years.

BoB had come across several transport ships scattered among the dunes, but they were nothing more than unrepairable wreckage and in far worse condition than Fixer's buried ship. At this point, Ala wasn't too terribly concerned about exploration, she just wanted to get to her starship and jump planet without a second glance back. The problem was that the path from their current location to the outpost station near her ship, would take them directly through the central base station terraformer complex. BoB warned her that the greatest concentration of hostile bots roamed that facility.

Trusting that they were now on friendly terms, Fixer returned her plasma rifle. He had cleaned it up as best as he could but did note that because of its age, there was always the possibility that it could misfire or lock up on her at any time. His own vessel was a cargo transport ship, so there were no munitions stored onboard. With the coming of another dawn, morning light sprinkled in through the bay door from *Shara*, first of the twin suns to rise; followed by *Kale* several hours later. These were the names the settlers had given their dual star system. Ala looked up this information on the ship's data logs with a tender smile as she learned their suns had been named after the daughter and son of their colony leader.

Ala felt a faint jerk at her heartstrings at that moment, she had always maintained a tough exterior, but she truly did miss her parents. On many long and lonely flights she caught herself wondering about her own future more than a few times, and the possibility of having a family of her own; but seedy spaceports and orbital stations were no place to raise a child …perhaps these colonists knew something after all.

She stuffed the small droids spare compartments as full as possible with compacted rations, to act as her pack mule. BoB didn't seem to mind, he appeared to be happy just to have something to do; any assignment to break the tedium of his existence. Ala tried to argue that she was willing to head to the main base station to possibly find better weaponry or a working surface vehicle to speed her on her journey, but BoB advised against it. She rationalized that the central hub would be better developed than the rest of the outlying areas, and thus, they would be safer from any alien critters roaming the arid tundra; and she didn't savor the idea of running into a swarm of giant bats out on the open terrain.

Ala wondered why they simply couldn't make contact

with any rogue bots in the area and just press her position of authority as a Controller, if push came to shove. Both BoB and Fixer, however, made her swallow the fact that prime directives were not something that could be easily bent or swayed. BoB had been protected from the anomaly that rewrote their programming, and Fixer had been mostly shielded and suffered only secondary effects. The bots who had been exposed to the full brunt of that storm might be another matter altogether, she realized, and affected in ways she had yet to fathom. There was no reason to be loitering in this derelict ship any longer, so BoB and Ala set out into the soft rays of the morning sun, leaving Fixer behind.

As they made their way out of the gully and across the dunes, she could tell life was still abundant here. They passed patches of plants spotting the landscape, many of which resembled Terran flowers, but eerily deformed. She had to admit that her new implant helped her feel better, processing the thin atmosphere to a much better degree. It was a peaceful trek through the midmorning until the 2nd sun, Kale, crept up over the horizon; dissipating a purple haze that stretched out across the skyline. Over a distant hill, Ala saw a flash of light and pointed it out to BoB who had been traveling beside her. As the glint of silver twinkled at them again, the droid motioned with his arm for her to keep low and out of sight behind the edge of the ridge.

"As I had feared, that appears to be a patrol up ahead," the droid whispered, "They are too far off to detect an FF signal, so we might as well wait until they pass; just to be safe," he advised.

Ala could hardly make out the figures in the distance and had assumed the bot must have a zoom lens equipped inside of his tin head. After an hour of waiting, the patrol had failed to budge; and true to character, that's when Ala started to get agitated.

"Look, Bob, maybe you can stand this heat, but I'm getting cooked out here," she stated while expressing her impatience. BoB had seen her shut down to low power before, but began to wonder if it was only possible for humans to enter sleep-mode during the night, "We should just skirt around them and get on our way," she finished.

"Unadvisable," BoB replied, "there are many different models of droids, and their individual sensory range is unknown to me. From my own experience, if you can see them, avoid them," he expressed with caution.

"Well, I'm not going to sit out here and fry in this heat," the girl protested, "I say we go around that rocky outcropping there," she pointed to their left at a score of vertical boulders, "…we can keep a visual on that group and continue on our merry way once we've passed them," Ala argued, much to the disgruntlement of the droid. Decisively, Ala got up and took off in the direction of the rocky outcropping, leaving BoB with no choice but to follow. With her soft-bodied shell, he wondered why she was prone to taking so many obvious risks.

The edge of the hill they were on emptied into what appeared to be a dry lake bed, now cracked and scarred by the heat of the twin suns. Just beyond it she could see the silhouette of a strange structure, a tall building surrounded by an interconnected jungle of pipes. Their path took them slightly closer to the patrol of bots, and Ala had a hard time making out what they were. She had recycled old worker droids from several abandoned colonies over the years but she didn't recognize any of these models as she caught glimpses of them through partitions in the rock they were hiking through.

She could hear them with her new implant, even at this range; it sounded as if they were talking in a form of chatter that traded rudimentary words, which seemed to be strung forwards and back without a clue to its context.

"Bob, what kind of droids are those, they seem awfully large," Ala asked under her breath.

"It would be wise to keep your speaker turned off until we are safely out of range," BoB whispered back, motioning her to keep silent. His repulsors hummed quietly as he made his way through the maze of rocks. Ala, though, was having a more difficult time with the terrain. Her curiosity got the better of her and eventually she failed to watch where she was stepping. The girl had to force herself to keep from screaming a string of obscenities when she jammed her bare toes upon a large jagged stone. She put her hand down to cover the bloody cut on her foot and set the rifle down so she could pamper the wound.

In his haste, BoB had failed to keep a visual on her. It wasn't until several moments later that he noticed that she wasn't on his trail. Backtracking, he found Ala tending her injured leg. With frozen shock, he watched as several silvery domes peered over the surrounding boulders down upon the prone girl, each with several glaring red eyes. Unwary to the situation, Ala turned her attention towards the bot, "I hurt myself like an idiot, I'm going to need your help here," she whispered to BoB while gritting her teeth. When the bot didn't move or respond, she shot a glance over to him and followed his line of sight to the crowd of silver bots surrounding them.

"I don't think you need to whisper anymore, Ala…" BoB finally answered.

One of the robots jumped down directly in front of the girl with a heavy *thump*, as Ala instinctively withdrew her legs; the shock of its landing knocked the rifle over, which dropped from her immediate reach. There was no escaping the half-dozen bots which had ambushed them. The large polished droid stood there, overshadowing the girl as sunlight glinted off its outer rim. Like Fixer, it had a multitude of eyes of various sizes speckled across its faceplate. Oddly enough, she noted that the thing looked vaguely like a giant chromed grasshopper; its two large gun barrels on either side of its head were pointing directly at her.

"FF determination scan unreadable, identify, what model are you?" The bots all asked as one, speaking the words in unison. The central bot shuffled with a few stomps of its two springy legs as BoB spoke from the edge of the outcropping.

"She isn't any model, she is a Controller," the small droid intervened at his own risk to save her. True to their appearance; when the bot had turned to face BoB, Ala could read the markings on its long back leg which read 'Cricket 7-B'. She had read the data file that the personnel on the Avalon project had imported insects to aid with pollination of their crops, but had the settlers been designing these outlandish robotic units for some strange agenda during their terraforming process? Using insects in agriculture she could understand; but making robots that resemble bugs made no sense at all.

She thought back to the small beetle-like droids she had first encountered after the night she awoke in the desert, but they didn't seem to serve any purpose either. These *Crickets* were armed with what appeared to be dual AG Cannons, which made them extremely dangerous; high caliber pulse guns such as these could create a lot of havoc, but she couldn't discern any function they could possibly serve in agriculture. These weren't worker droids, they were designed for combat.

"A Controller?" The Crickets all asked in unison with a tone of confusion. She could tell some were slightly smaller models marked as 7-A, with the alphabetical letters apparently used as a reference to their size. The largest, 7-C model, overlooked the scene from a distance, its dual guns still locked in the firing mode. BoB scooted forward, his clamp arm set back within his housing to keep from appearing as a threat. At that instant there was a brief hum in the air Ala could discern from her implant, but couldn't hear with her ears.

"FF neutral; no faction yet assigned," the bot in the center stated; at that notice, the surrounding Crickets retracted their AG barrels. They were anti-gun munitions that could shoot a narrow pulse of sonic waves and were capable of some serious armor penetration. BoB drifted over to the girl as the bots kept their eyes on him.

"Are you damaged?" He asked Ala, who nodded back to BoB with a worried smile.

"We have no need of resources; we merely wish to pass through this sector. We intend no harm to you," BoB addressed the Crickets, trying his best to be diplomatic.

"Negative, all enemy units entering this sector are to be deactivated," the central bot answered as BoB and Ala gave each other a worried glance, "and all unaffiliated units are to be secured for scanning. The Controller model must also be brought in to be categorized," the chromed bot ordered.

"But, I am a Controller," Ala responded smugly, "...I order you to let us go."

"You do not *control* us, Controller," the bot responded back flatly, leaving a blank look of dismay upon her face.

Now prisoners, the two companions were instructed to accompany the hostile droids to the base at the far end of the dry lake bed. Even though they were warned to not try any attempt at escape, Ala realized these remarkably customized droids could far outmaneuver either of them if they should try to flee. As her foot was injured, Ala was advised to climb upon one of the Cricket droids; and without much warning, she was forced to hang on for dear life.

Her mount sprung several dozen feet into the air to clear the boulder field, and even higher to clear several hundred feet with each successive leap. The thick hinge that connected their legs to the bodies was rimmed with a mesh of alloy rubber webbing that absorbed the shock of landing. As Ala lay clinging upon the smooth back of the machine, she could hear internal gears and pistons wind and whir before each jump.

The other bots joined them through the aerial acrobatics; Ala got a brief view of the surrounding landscape as the wind whipped through her hair. Behind them, the last pair of crickets escorted BoB along the surface. The base ahead was a series of large pipes that stretched around the central complex and intertwined into a confused dance of ducts and conduits. From its center, a pair of deep channels emptied far out into a dry bay. Most likely, this was one of the pumping stations the colonists had once used for water filtration runoff. The entire skin of the facility was covered in a dark brown rust, giving it an imposing air of gloom.

The area around the complex itself was bustling with activity. Bots of every size were scurrying about on individual errands; there were even humongous disc-shaped robots that resembled beetles hauling large containers full of scrap metal. Ala's escort came to a halt at the entrance of the walled facility in front of several armored droids armed with automated guns lined atop the front gate. Again, she felt that strange silent hum in the air as they transferred their friend or foe signal to the front sentry. With a grind, the tall double doors swung open to allow them entry. The young pilot was surprised to see several robots stop dead in their tracks to stare at her with acute curiosity. Those that had flexible heads turned them to watch as she was escorted into the belly of the industrial complex.

She noticed the giant disk-shaped beetles had a bronze tint to them, with a bold white 'T' marked across their tops. There were a few as merely as tall as she, to those that were of gargantuan size. Towering above all the other droids, these robotic goliaths trudged directly over them. With all this AI technology at hand, Ala was surprised to see that the inside of the facility was just as deteriorated as the tarnished exterior. It was clear that these bots had made no effort to perform any maintenance on the buildings they utilized. Within, a jungle of rusted pipes led from ceiling to floor in an array of countless conduits and pressure valves. As advanced as the complex was, it was apparent that everything here had been offline for quite some time.

Ala was ushered into an oval room with an operation table that looked similar to the one back on Fixer's ship, only much larger; which made Ala a little apprehensive about getting near it. The Cricket instructed two other insect-like bots in the room to analyze her, and Ala was left in their care. With her wounded foot there was certainly no way she was going to make a run for it, let alone vault the high wall surrounding the complex, The pair of technician robots turned to one another and promptly produced a glowing conduit that looked nearly identical to the one Fixer had used to subdue her.

"Oh, you've got to be shitting me…" Ala blurted out as they struck her with the probe, which immediately knocked her unconscious with a violent jolt.

She awoke again without any clue as to how much time had drained away while she was passed out. With heavy eyelids, she looked wearily about the room. The two tech droids had clamped her onto the wall for inspection. An odd machine shaped vaguely like an hourglass sat in front of her, using a web of lasers to record her dimensions and taking other sensor readings. The two bug droids seemed to be arguing about the results of the analysis and deciding if they should pry her shell open to view her internal circuitry. Ala tried to speak, but coughed on her first draw of breath, which caused the scan to cease as her movement interrupted the process.

"I'm not a droid, nor a machine," she spat at them, "I'm a Controller …or so I was told," Ala added with a hint of disdain. One of the bugs came up to her and inspected her closely with its antenna stalked eyes.

"But you are *part* machine," it retorted as if phrased in a question, as it pointed to her arm, "the rest of your design is uncategorized, and your model seems to have been created within banned guidelines," it added.

"So what?" Ala answered wearily.

"So, this is unacceptable, as your current design model is forbidden and must be revised to meet acceptable parameters," the bot answered blandly as its colleague waved its antennae in agreement.

"What the hell does that mean?" Ala inquired with a squeak as she received the answer she feared.

"Your shell must be upgraded. So we must decide whether to remove or add a few new limbs, and the same must go for your sensor interface on your headpiece. We might as well detach your memory core and refit it into one of our current robotic units," the tech answered in a casual tone as it debated the prospects with its colleague.

Ala got that sinking feeling in her stomach; these things were planning to cut her up and make her into a cybernetic monstrosity! The bot at the table took a short moment to decide on which tool to use and approached the girl with a sharp instrument to pry her open. Ala stared back in horror as she fought the urge to faint.

"Stop, wait!" She tried to stall out of desperation, "You will only damage my internal …uh, custom circuitry," she tried to reason.

"We don't understand," the insect bot turned to its companion, "…you do not wish to be upgraded? It inquired with a note of confusion.

"I am not created to any set parameters," Ala cried as tears welled in her eyes. She was about to be diced up and put back together like a sonic toaster, "I'm human … *we made you*, you stupid machines!" Ala shot back, letting her temper get the best of her, which wasn't all that unusual for her whenever she felt afraid. The two bugs looked at one another, their optical antennae waving with unease.

"You possess no encoded parameters?" The closest one asked with mild shock. The pair of droids weren't programmed to decipher lies, so they took her word at full value. At that, they started to bicker among themselves at the implication of her claim, as Ala vainly tugged at her restraints while they were distracted. After half an hour, both technician bots finally cane to a mutual agreement that Ala must have suffered a major core malfunction and should be entirely dismantled, and then reprogrammed with the proper operational codes.

'Great going, Ala'; she thought to herself with a sigh of resignation.

It was then that a large metallic spider crawled into the room. Compared to the other bots, this one looked brand new, as its shell was polished black steel and spotless compared to most of the bots she had seen cavorting around the complex. It had three long legs that ended in dagger-sharp lances. It had a small ST-C lettering with a string of numbers stamped along its side. Two small cannon barrels were mounted on its raised dome, accompanied by a pair of extremely vicious-looking arched pincers. Ala guessed this was the medical bot assigned to dice her up and gut her for spare parts; it certainly looked like it could do the job. The large spider-bot spoke with an authoritative tone, getting the immediate attention of the two tech droids in the lab.

"Have you finished analyzing this unit?" It demanded.

"Well, yes, but this sentient unit is being uncooperative and we currently recommend that it be dismantled and reprogrammed with the proper base directives," the pair of bots suggested.

"Negative, you are hereby ordered to release this unit into my custody ...unaltered," the spider instructed after a short pause. The two bot technicians looked at one another with their waving antennae for a brief moment, as if boggled by the demand.

"But ...this unit is clearly in violation of our primary directive!" the bolder of the two stated. The large spider stepped towards the two smaller technicians while clacking its sharp pincers. The two techs clearly showed fear at the menacing gesture, each taking a step back on their multiple legs.

"This order is not to be countermanded, Tech!" It growled, "This unit is to be used as valued collateral against the opposing factions," it demanded. At that, the two tech droids lowered their antenna eyes in submission and scurried over to release Ala from her restraints. Dropping to the floor completely naked, the girl took a moment to gather her strength as her limbs had gone numb from being strapped to the wall. She wasn't sure if she was in much better company now, but it was certainly preferable to being dismembered. She had been a mere hair's breadth from being chopped apart by a bunch of psychotic robots; what a fucking nightmare this planet had turned out to be.

After they freed her, the two techs continued to argue between themselves in hushed tones; clearly trying to avoid the oppressive gaze of the robotic spider's multiple eyes. They were simple technician bots and used to taking orders, and clearly had no form of offensive capabilities as many of the other droids possessed. Apparently, the fear for self-preservation was deeply engrained into them as it had been encoded into their databanks. They knew that resources were limited, and fear of being deactivated and gutted for parts was a real threat to any bot that failed to perform its assigned duties, whether they agreed to it or not.

The spider stood aside and retracted its razor-sharp mandibles so as not to appear threatening to the girl. This stumped Ala for a moment, as she thought she was a prisoner. Halfway out the door, she remembered to grab

Michel Savage

her mesh skirt left crumpled on the ground. With the heavy clacking of its metal legs on the floor, the looming spider followed closely behind her, guiding Ala out towards the exit. The scared girl was justifiably worried about what was to become of her.

"Where are you taking me?" She asked timidly with a glance over her shoulder. Without breaking stride, the spider answered in a familiar voice.

"It's me Ala, Bah-b," the bot answered to her utter surprise, "The moment I was taken in, they dismantled my shell and refitted my core into this upgraded model," BoB explained to her relief; but after a few wandering moments of thought, Ala became a little troubled about what that might possibly mean.

Wastelands

Ala gave a brief sigh of relief once they cleared the front entry, but they still had to make their way past the gate. Instead of heading towards the sentries at the main entrance, BoB instructed her to skirt the building towards the far side of the complex. In the back, several hulking robots were busy hauling salvaged metal and dropping them in dump pits where the scrap was being sorted.

"Bob, where are you taking us?" Ala asked with a worried glance.

"I would advise that we keep personal communications to a minimum until we are outside the complex, Ala," he warned, which assured her he was still on her side.

BoB found what he was looking for at the far end of the salvage dump; an opening to the lower drainage tunnels. While no one was looking, he instructed her to grasp onto his chassis while he slipped down the shaft. They were immediately enveloped by darkness, and all of BoB's multiple red eyes lit up; illuminating the corridor with just enough light for her to see.

"This was a drainage vent once used to purge the filtration tanks; we can use it to escape from the other end, which opens into the lake bed beyond," the droid advised as they swiftly made their way through the dreary tunnel.

"I don't understand, Bob, didn't they reprogram you after they refitted you into …that?" Ala asked, referring to his new shell.

"When I was brought into the facility, I computed the likelihood of that event; my original model was a much older design and I was able to manually disengage my core memory chips just before I was refitted," BoB explained as the clacking of his spider legs tapped through the sand-filled passage, "Before they disposed of my old shell, I was able to recover the rations you required for your energy needs," he added to her relief, opening a small compartment to allow her to grab a sealed pouch of water stashed within.

"But how did you know this tunnel was here, and you played a pretty hard bluff back there; I thought you said bots couldn't lie," Ala asked her companion, and was anticipating what answer he would offer for that change of protocol he supported so stubbornly.

"I didn't say droids *couldn't* deceive, I simply stated that we don't," BoB responded flatly, "When you brought up the introduction of new peripherals about uses of deceit and their possible applications, I stored that useful information and utilized that tactic when it was required."

"You mean I taught you..." she started to say before BoB interrupted her.

"...Yes Ala, you helped me learn how to lie," he stated, and Ala didn't exactly know if that was something she should be proud of, but it did save her ass. The droid continued with his explanation, "When my memory core was refitted into this new shell they also added fresh circuitry and reformatted the newly installed memory banks. It wasn't until I was brought back online again that I connected and rebooted my internal chips that were shielded during the process," the bot added to help her understand, "This new body was also upgraded with the schematics of this facility, and I came to find you as soon as I could," he finished at length, hoping that would answer her inquiry.

"But, Bob, couldn't they tell that you weren't one of them?" Ala asked curiously, noting that the two repair techs had apparently sealed up the open cut on her foot with a clear film adhesive; at least it didn't hurt anymore.

As they made their way towards the pinhole of light at the end of the tunnel, BoB tried to explain the best he could in words she would understand. His new body had also been uploaded with all relevant data on the present global situation on Tranquility.   BoB himself was surprised to discover that the other bots had erased their own data cores so frequently, that all their original programming had been deleted long ago. It was at such an extent that most of them didn't even recognize human life forms as their original Controllers, especially since none had been seen for several decades. He tried to explain this wasn't all that uncommon for bots to delete unnecessary blocks of memory but apparently, it had been taken to the extreme. Without the presence of Controllers to update their routine programs, the humans themselves were simply forgotten; and all memory of their existence was eventually eradicated.

The bots in this sector and those that surrounded the main complex had escalated both their conflict and their modifications far beyond what he could have imagined. Apparently, there were now several large clusters of bots that had broken into separate warring factions, attacking each other for the limited resources that were left. The farming harvesters, mining robots, and numerous other types of droids had splintered into self-sustaining groups. BoB couldn't fully understand the social breakdown. For some reason, all the bots that had been exposed to that freak storm that destroyed the human colony decades ago were now evolving at their own drawn initiative.

There was no present need to continue mining ores, or drilling wells, or harvesting the agriculture as the bots had no need to waste time growing food or creating such material comforts. Accessing the data spool in his new body, BoB revealed that by some force, the bots converged soon after the cataclysm and found no need to continue the operations they had performed for the human settlers that were no longer present, and they slowly separated into savage gangs that preyed on weaker bots for their energy cores and spare parts. As more of the bots were activated and recruited, it escalated into the present chaos as these once placid droids began to war against one another.

In reflection, Ala realized the population of bots had been tainted by one of the most undesirable human traits of all. While encoding their core primary directives for self-preservation, mankind itself had cursed these bots toward their own annihilation. These droids could only recycle what limited knowledge they had been originally programmed with and could not fabricate new forms of energy, nor perform the maintenance required for existing resources. In their binary logic, they reverted to what they had learned from the inherent traits of their previous masters; to take from others and survive without consideration or regard for who or what they destroyed in the process. That character flaw made these robots far more human than Ala cared to acknowledge.

When they reached the far end of the tunnel, her eyes adjusted back to the bright sunlight. The exit was blocked by a thick portcullis, and BoB required Ala's assistance to raise the rusted gate that had a manual wheel built for use by human hands. She latched the gate in place once it was up far enough for them to escape, but noticed the wheel lock was only accessible from the interior; which was why it had remained unguarded.

Keeping out of sight, they skirted the edge of the banks of the dry lakebed until they found a slope gentle enough for Ala to climb. Although BoB's new body was large enough to carry her, she found his domed top far too slippery, and that he had the tendency to lurch with jerky movements with the three legs his model was equipped with. Ala thought the spider casing was actually an inefficient design because the droid would be rendered immobile if even one of his legs became damaged. She did have to wonder why these bots were fashioned to resemble insects and why she hadn't seen any that fly like airships or used magnetic repulsors as BoB's old rusted unit had. It would certainly have seemed more efficient, especially considering the difficult terrain.

The droid had to explain that such anti-gravitational devices had strict limitations on the amount of weight they could sustain, and the native droids had no ability to forge such technology without the proper schematics.

"I may have dumped a lot of my own memory over the years, but these customized robotic units were not originally created by the controllers of this settlement. This drastic self-remodeling we have witnessed, is from something far more recent," BoB admitted, and Ala tended to agree that she had never seen anything like them before. Such outlandishly designed droids wouldn't be of any practical use to a blooming colony that needed every spare bot for labor and land development. No matter how she put the question, BoB could not give a straight answer as to why these rogue bots had chosen to model themselves after the likeness of insects; it was all very strange.

The young scavy wondered if it might be worth backtracking to find the weapons she had left behind when they had been captured, but BoB strongly advised against it. Since he had been fitted with a new shell, his tracking sensors had been stripped; that and his original positioning systems logs had been removed during his installment into this new body. Making an attempt to retrieve her lost plasma rifle might not only be a waste of time but might possibly end up getting them recaptured. He also made a point to her that if that were to happen, his recent actions of presenting falsehoods to the other bots would likely be diagnosed as a faulty installment; and he would be promptly dismantled to every nut and bolt and decommissioned as scrap parts.

Ala felt even more naked without a gun and had to rely on BoB's new armaments for their defense. After asking how he liked his new body, the droid let her know in so many unfettered words that he was still trying to get used to it. The spider tank C series was a relatively small mobile unit in comparison to the other bots; it had a rotating dome separated from its central ring that connected its three long legs. BoB spat out the model specs from the installed data spool. His body was armed with one forward Arch Cannon and a rear AG gun, which he timidly expressed he was afraid to test; and doing so now would most likely draw unwanted attention.

There was also a sub-compartment located at its base containing a cache of mines. BoB admitted he had not yet run a full diagnostic as to exactly how they worked, as he had been in far too much of a hurry to escape. To do so, he would have to power down for several hours while he labeled the root systems; even then it would merely be a summary of how each of the weapons functioned rather than actually seeing them in action. Nevertheless, Ala felt a bit safer with a walking tank beside her.

These bug-like bots were not entirely fresh creations; the droids simply used a creative combination of parts from several different types of worker droids that had been pieced together into these new designs. The moving force behind their incentive to do so was the real mystery here. BoB felt entirely lost; for the first time he was without his tracking sensors, and it clearly disturbed him to the point where he showed a severe lack of confidence as to where he was leading them. Ala, on the other hand, retained her sense of direction and recognized the horizon to which they were heading.

The distant haze did not hide the unmistakable triple-pronged towers of the central terraformer, reaching high into the sky like a sculpted crown. The main facility was enormous, as it was the hub to which all the vital facilities were connected. Unfortunately, that was where the leading faction of the rogue droids had taken refuge. It sat there like a black widow in the center of its web, waiting to consume anyone who drew too near. Even so, Ala presumed that was the only place she would find any real answers.

The landscape was covered with fields of sand dunes spotted with alien shrubbery and rocky outcroppings that helped provide a shady oasis from the scorching heat. As the two companions looked out over the sea of sand, the gas giant Thebes began to rise from the horizon like a celestial tidal wave. To her relief, the giant planet soon eclipsed the larger of the two suns. Noticing a flare of light, Ala saw something glint in the distance. While fearing it might be more patrol bots, BoB had to reassure her that his sensors were not picking up any movement from the area ahead.

Any man-made structure was worth investigating, so they took a minor detour to inspect the odd building. It was dark in color, though it glimmered at them from the angle of the setting sun. What appeared to have been a toppled tower from a distance turned out to be another crashed transport ship, though of a different class than the one Fixer had occupied. This one was deeply embedded in the sand at a steep angle, a tell-tale sign as to how violent the initial impact must have been.

They approached the wreck cautiously, though BoB could still not detect any movement within. Once they got alongside the vessel, they found many marks in the dirt and clear signs that the local droids had been busy stripping whatever they could from the hull. The side docking hatch was currently half buried under the shifting sand, and BoB's bladed pincers were quite useless for digging. From the faded markings on its side, Ala could read that this was once a personnel transport ship. This was only one of a few space-worthy vehicles that would have been used to evacuate the planet. Obviously, this one hadn't made it.

Likely, the bridge had been crushed upon impact, but the hull of the passenger compartment was still sound. Digging by hand in the shadow of the hull, Ala made an effort to free the compartment hatch so she could take a look inside. If she was lucky, there might be a plasma rifle or two and some real clothing for her to wear. Helpless in the task, BoB wandered to a short distance to scan the horizon and act as lookout in case any hostile droids approached the area.

She was still sweating like a dog when she scraped away the last handfuls of sand, and she gave the door a hard yank. With a grinding creak, the hatch resisted at first but swung open with a clang when she put her weight into it. It was dead quiet within, silent except for the whistling of the wind through the weathered cracks in the hull.

"Ala," BoB called to her from a distance as she was about to take her first step within, and paused to look back to see his turret spin towards her, "…I think you should come here for a moment to see this."

Wiping the dirt from her hands, the young pilot tromped over to the metal spider to see what he was looking at. There, scattered among the hollow of a windswept dune lay several dozen human skulls; piled upon one another in a heap of carnage. It took Ala several moments to realize that there were no bodies attached to them, these people had been decapitated and their heads left scattered here like refuse. Ala was horrified. These colonists were not victims of the crash but had been brutally murdered. She stood there gazing over the sad scene until she couldn't look anymore and turned away; so this was the fate of the settlers. There was no question of it now, the rogue bots must have been responsible for this carnage.

Ala walked back to the open hatch with a sick feeling. A new light had been cast on the true nature of these wild bots and what they were capable of. She remembered BoB's analogy that repetitive memory dumps were the reason why the droids had not killed her the moment she was captured and acted as though they didn't even know what she was. Three decades is not a great length of time to be so forgetful, unless of course, your memory had been frequently erased over such a span. Even if confronted with this atrocity, would any of them remember what had happened here?

BoB tiptoed behind her on his spindly legs so he could stand guard back at the door of the ship. Ala bent her head and stepped inside. The stale air had an unpleasant tinge to it. Carefully, she climbed her way down the angled corridor, finding few handholds to grasp onto in the consuming darkness. It took several moments for her eyes to adjust to the dim light pouring through the open hatch. She wasn't looking for food or survivors, but a weapon and a jumpsuit, or even a pair of boots would be nice to find.

The interior had deteriorated at an accelerated rate under these arid environmental conditions, but she also noted strange large gashes in the corridor frames and blackened patches of soot along the walls. She checked any cabinet she could pry open but found nothing of useful value. Climbing down the aisle to the bottom angle of the hold, she found hundreds of passenger chairs bolted to the walls and floor. To her horror, she discovered one seat occupied by a headless corpse, then across the hall, yet another body. Many of the launch seats had been sheared apart, right through their composite steel frames.

In the darkness, she stepped on something that cracked beneath her feet. At the bottom section of the ship, the dim threads of light from the open hatch above slowly illuminated a ghastly scene. Ala's breath caught in her throat as she peered up from the human arm she had crushed beneath her foot, as her gaze drifted over to the large heap of intertwined bodies.

Several of the colonists were headless, many more were torn to shreds, or their skin burned into melted dried lumps. Those few skulls among the pile had their flesh stretched over their faces, their jaws agape in a silent scream. Her head felt suddenly dizzy, and Ala caught herself from fainting and risk falling into the pile of corpses to join in their grisly embrace. The smoky scent she had smelled before was the lingering stench of their cooked and seared flesh.

Ala turned around to get out of there as fast as she could when something caught her eye; a silver barrel of a firearm lying among the charred remains. With a degree of hesitation, she lowered herself closer to the pile of dead. Moving a scorched arm, Ala pried the pulse gun out of the corpse's grasp. To her horror, the arm broke off in her hand as the body fell to the side; exposing a dead robot lying beneath.

This droid was different and not designed after any insect as far as she could tell. It was near human height, with one single large eye surrounded by a hood of metal. One of its arms was thick like an oversized gun barrel; the other was shaped like a scythe blade over a yard long. A chill ran up her spine as she thought about what it had been used for. There was a white stamp in the center of its chest plate, marking a capital G; the rest of its body was buried under the pile of corpses, which was little consolation for the victims. Luckily, the strange droid was deactivated and dead.

It was obvious that most of the bodies had been severely burned by something other than mere crossfire combat. At least the pulse gun she found was worth taking; she would have to get it topside to see if it was damaged in any way. Ala realized there might be more weapons buried in this mess, but she wasn't about to go digging through the mound of rotting dead.

It was a steep climb, but Ala finally made her way to the top, nearly huffing for breath in the stagnant air. To Ala, reaching the doorway out of that dark hole was like being baptized in sunlight; washing away the cold terror that lay sleeping within the crypt below. BoB's legs skittered as he turned when he saw her at the cabin door.

"What did you find?" He asked, shifting his dome with curiosity, as no insect model robot could possibly fit through the small hatch door. Ala tried to shake off what she had just seen.

"There must be more than a hundred dead bodies littering the ship, the colonists inside were slaughtered like fucking pigs. What a nightmare..." Ala spoke with a hollow tone as she stepped through the hatch and out into the warm sunlight to shake off the chill. She inspected the gun she had recovered for any defects. It was a meager low-grade weapon, but certainly better than nothing. As the setting suns were beginning to sink on the horizon, the two companions continued their way towards the spires in the distance, leaving the dead ship and the forgotten tragedy it held to the drifting sands.

*   *   *

Behind the rusted hatch, down within the dark recesses of the derelict transport shuttle; the pile of bodies slowly began to twitch from beneath. A soft red glow flickered to life in the single eye of the murderous android model known as the Hellbot; a name it had rightfully earned.

Bot Wars

Ala and her companion were making good time towards the base station, their plan was to reach the outer perimeters and follow one of the adjoining junctions. Since BoB had his tracking sensors removed entirely and Ala lost the map she had scratched upon her axe, it was the best they could do for the moment. If they could reach Outpost 9, or better yet, possibly find a functional communications array so she could call her ship; it would save them a great deal of added grief. Considering recent events, the young pilot began to wonder if her spacecraft was still sitting where she had left it.

There was always the chance that a droid scouting party might have happened upon it and decided to tear the Valkyrie apart for scrap metal. Ala doubted the onboard AI would allow such a thing, but she had not left Valaria with any final instructions before she got shanghaied into the middle of nowhere. She would be devastated if they got to the target outpost and she found nothing left of her ship but a ravaged shell. The worry of that began to weigh heavily upon her shoulders and prompted Ala with a renewed sense of urgency.

The Valkyrie was equipped with automated defenses, but they were entirely meager at best; built to be not much more than a deterrent. If any heavily armed bot happened to get pissed off by the paltry defenses, it might likely blast a hole in her ship; causing a mortal hull breach she would be unable to repair. A slew of such scenarios flipped through Ala's head as she crossed the hot sand to the point the stress of it was eating away at her. To keep herself from dwelling on it, she asked BoB to tell her about the types of droids they had seen. All of their specifications had been installed within his new body, information which could be of tactical value.

"I've told you about the model I was installed with," BoB mentioned, referring to himself, "but I still need to take the time to run a full diagnostic to determine its full scope of operation. Hold on, let me access the data spool," he added after a moment, "Our captors were the Cricket series which are known as jumpers for obvious reasons, the current models are 7a through 7c…"

"What do the numbers means?" Ala interrupted, as they made their way towards the spires.

"The alphabetical letters apparently correspond with size; the number means it is the 7th generation design since the first prototype of the model." BoB responded, "They are equipped with dual forward cannons and a track of short-range mini-bombs stored within their rear compartments," the droid continued, "The larger T series that are designed to resemble beetles are utilized as shields, they are equipped with a single proton cannon and primarily used to breach blockades and deployed as effective fire cover for smaller units in combat situations. These heavy units are highly valued and take a great deal of resources to build," he added.

"So, all these bots are primarily being built to serve as soldiers?" Ala inquired.

"Affirmative, although they double as lookouts and scouts, and call in service droids who act as foragers," he relayed. "Also logged within my core is the R series known as a Mantis, which is used in both salvage and sentry operations; but its record status states that it has no ranged weapons equipped on its current model, only possessing a pair of titanium claws," BoB reported, "Ah, in reflection, that was the robot model that was hunting me the first night we both met; do you remember, Ala?" the droid recalled. She had thought it was a native animal of some sort, but now understood why she heard the screeching of metal as the creature made its way through the silos. It also must have been responsible for destroying the smaller beetles she had found scattered about the area the next morning.

"There is also a fascinating model listed here, which are referred to as Night Crawlers. It is recorded as having three sets of laser cannons and the ability to create a short-ranged electromagnetic pulse discharge, as its specialty weapon to disable foes."

"Interesting, I've yet to see one of those," Ala added, "is thereby chance any log of a 'G' series or robot model listed among your archives?" She had to ask as her mind wandered back to the dead humanoid robot she had recently seen in the crashed shuttle a few hours before.

"One moment, accessing…" BoB paused, "actually, there is only a sub-log about a G series, but it appears that model has been recalled for quite some time."

"Do you still have the specs on it, Bob?" She asked with a slight shiver.

"Searching..." he paused again while scanning for the data, "the G series were manufactured from the parts of the mounted Guardian defense system, which was originally constructed to protect the settlement from raiders, profiteers, or any other unwelcome riffraff that might ever attack the colony," the droid enlightened her. "Most interesting …since this G series was clearly in violation of their new prime directive, as they were not modeled after insects at all, but were built close to standard human dimensions so they could…"

"So they could hunt down the colonists," the girl intervened as a cold look washed across her face while BoB shifted his dome with a troubled glance at her. It made sense; whatever force was behind the robot rebellion chose to make one exception in its primary laws and created man-sized bots that could track down the colonists wherever they might hide. After several steps in silence and a measure of apprehension, BoB continued reading the specs to her.

"They were equipped with a fully integrated artificial intelligence, a single standard pulse rifle built into one of its limbs along with a blade and flame thrower used for incinerating debris," BoB continued.

'Debris, huh?' Ala thought to herself as she shook her head in disgust to the curt reference of humans as trash.

"The defense manufacturer for the Guardian was the same one who created the original '**HEL**' system, or military-grade **H**igh **E**nergy **L**aser, as it was known. It was a devastating weapon that was the primary cause of the elevated casualty rate during the 4th world war that escalated throughout the entire Terran system," BoB enlightened her while reading the sub files on the data spool, "Thus, these models were coined as the Hellbots; though to date, the G series are no longer in production. The closed log says they were officially christened as the *Reaper* …which is a reference I am not quite familiar with," BoB admitted with a quizzical glance at the girl.

It was becoming incrementally clear that the destruction of this colony was willful and intentional; but who was behind it, and why? If another corporate competitor planted a virus into their computer systems to sabotage the Avalon project, then why hadn't they laid claims to their prize or its salvage rights after all these years? Maybe the timing of that freak storm was just a coincidence …or maybe not.

"There is also an extensive list of upgraded droids in present commission," BoB continued in stride, "such as the model 88, which…" the spider droid came to a sudden halt and Ala looked over to see a pronged antenna extend from the top of his domed shell, "I sense motion ahead of us, Ala," BoB whispered in alarm.

A collection of steep hills had funneled their passage down into a low valley as they neared the central sector. Ala could see several large metallic objects moving across their projected path. There was no need to send out an FF signal, as doing so would compromise their position. Ala stroked the pulse gun she had confiscated, its energy bar was nearly depleted, and she doubted it would do much good against the heavily armored bots she had seen. It was only a close-range weapon and she didn't plan on putting the firearm to the test so soon.

With as much stealth as possible, they made their way across the windswept field of sand and rock. The double sunset would be coming soon; as Kale, the smaller of the two suns, was lowering to the horizon once again. The gas giant was nearing its equinox and would eclipse the small moon in a matter of hours. The esteemed REVO Corporation must have chosen this planet for its near-Earth mean gravity, because it certainly wasn't for these wildly eccentric daylight hours they had to endure.

With his antenna out, BoB was picking up a great deal of radio traffic. They saw a large mass of bots converge in the distance. BoB spun his shell around and began picking up significantly more digital noise; something was amiss.

"If I'm not mistaken, an incursion is about to commence, and we are not exactly in the best place for such and engagement at the moment," BoB advised. The droid was correct; they were locked in the low valley surrounded by steep hills, "There are two warring factions about to converge in this sector in a feudal claim for territory," BoB informed the girl while he was deciphering the digital signals, "There is a good chance they might not detect you because you are organic, but their sensors will likely catch my movements …I'm not exactly as small as I once was," he reminded her.

"What should we do?" Ala asked, feeling a bit nervous.

"We should try to make it to the edge of the valley if we can; their sensors might be blocked by the terrain if we're able to skirt around the edge of the hillside. I need to find someplace safe to shut down so they don't detect my power signature," the droid explained.

Making their way as quickly as possible from the swarm of droids coalescing, the two companions headed for the edge of the far hill. Its steep rocky slopes were too smooth for even Ala to climb, so they desperately tried to find a pile of boulders that would hide them from view and detection by radar sensors. Unfortunately, they never got the chance to make it that far. A swarm of droids came rolling over the hill behind them from the pumping station they had recently escaped from. Luck befell them when the automated ping of their FF signals spotted BoB as one of their own, and the column proceeded towards the approaching mass of enemy robots at the far end of the valley. The two opposing armies came to a sudden halt for a still moment as the air filled with negative pings. Ala was about to behold an epic battle no human had ever witnessed before.

Like a celestial signal from the gods themselves, the gas giant, Thebes, took but moments to eclipse the setting sun as it rolled across the sky. A dark shadow fell across the valley as thousands of red eyes lit upon the battlefield. Through her implant, Ala could feel the tension in the air radiating like an electrical aura.

It started with a single shot. Before the first beam of plasma hit, it was followed by a salvo of tracer rounds and a volley from their mounted arch cannons. True to their name, the curved jets of plasma exploded over the enemy line, sending a rain of shrapnel in the form of primed particles down upon the opposing troops. A few stray rounds struck the rocks where Ala stood and she to scramble for cover. There were bots of every size, metallic insects scouring over the field in mortal combat.

Fire from energy cannons tore through the front lines, ripping gears and appendages from their hosts. Lasers burned through the field of robots, cutting them down in short bursts. The other side dished back what they received, along with a luminescent spray of repeating fire from ion cannons and static pulse guns. Ala had never seen such savagery; each bot fighting for its own survival, each one a living weapon.

All school children were taught about the last world war, which had wiped out over half the human race on Terra Prime and escalated across the Sol solar system to Earth's outlying planets. Neither moon bases nor the colonies on Mars had escaped the carnage that scarred the lives of every man, woman, and child during that bloody era. That appalling time in human history had been thoroughly recorded, however, the preserved videos and images of the war itself were censored from modern media. Those horrific scenes weren't something most decent people would want to see anyhow as we hid our true history in shame from future generations. It was truly the lowest point in mankind's existence in the universe, an embarrassing reminder of the insanity and cruelty we were capable of.

The stain of our violent civilization was being relived here on this shattered battlefield. Ala and her droid companion scurried for cover from explosions and flying debris that whistled in their direction. More than once an enemy bot spotted BoB in their sights, only to be gutted or blown to bits when they turned to deliver a volley of fire at his position. BoB himself received several dents and burns as pulse rounds ricocheted off his shell in his effort to protect Ala as best he could.

The T model beetle juggernauts lurched slowly forward like massive giants, taking the brunt of the arch cannon fire as they protected their troops who rallied beneath their protective shells. Infrequently, one of these goliaths would be taken down when their thick pillared legs were blown out from beneath them. For the first time, Ala saw the R model mantis in action. These tall bots swarmed forward as shock troops, climbing over the enemy lines to cleaving apart heads and limbs with their titanium claws. Without ranged weaponry of their own, they relied on their speed to evade hostile fire. Through the flash of explosions, Ala and her spider droid made their way as fast as they could towards the exit of the valley, screaming directions towards one another over the raging thunder of the weapons fire.

In the heat of the battle, Ala finally saw the source of the devastating energy cannons. Robotic scorpions skittered forward and braced to absorb the recoil as bursts of hot yellow beams flashed from their twin pincers; followed by a shower of laser fire from their poised tails overhead. She watched as their low profile worked against them the moment a shield beetle smashed one under its giant metal leg; crushing it to bits. These monolithic walking shields with they're equipped proton cannons were the grand fireworks of the battle; spouting a single hollow beam of hot energy followed by a spinning coil of purged ions was eerily beautiful to watch as it was equally fascinating to witness such murderous devastation.

When the concentrated blast of gamma radiation hit a bot, its shell would literally blur as its very atoms lost cohesion; the beam cut into its shell, exploding it from within. Then streamers of purged ions would follow, creating a blazing shower of sparks flying from the point of impact. Clouds of thick black smoke rose within fireballs into the fading night sky. As she held her small pulse gun tightly in her grip, Ala felt helpless against such destructive firepower, knowing that at any moment a stray laser could cut her in two.

She took refuge under the colossal broken shell of a giant bot that had tumbled free of the main fray. Her spider droid companion coiled in his legs to fit within the hollow beside her, protecting the girl from live rounds and flying shrapnel. Taking cover, they both watched as several C class spider droids, identical to BoB, flitted across the battlefield, almost dancing between the enemy units with their unique agility. Like a strike tank, they advanced forward; taking out damaged or wounded opponents with their AG cannons, and in timed unison, they came to a sudden halt behind the enemy lines.

The spiders all stood erect, high on their appendages for a few brief seconds as enemy fire dashed between their thin legs; then suddenly their main bodies dropped hard to the ground. BoB was even more fascinated than the girl to watch what happened next. "Most interesting..." BoB whispered as they observed lower hatch doors that opened on opposite sides of the spider tanks, and a literal swarm of dozens of mobile mines, that resembled miniature versions of the arachnids, emptied from the holding compartment and spread across the battlefield. After releasing their load, their parent versions picked themselves up to escape back across the battle line; although several units never made it that far before succumbing to enemy counter fire.

The swarm of tiny spider mines spaced themselves and locked immobile, becoming indiscernible from the field of debris around them. The enemy bots in the forefront who had witnessed the release, were hesitant to step into the field but were forced forward by the advancing surge from the rear. Bots who stepped past them had their legs blown off and thrown high into the air, the thundering report was deafening. Retreating troops received the same treatment, many seeking refuge behind their own lines, but never reaching it as they would lose one limb, only to make a fatal stumble onto another hidden mine.

Ala was confused and bewildered, for unlike any other war that she had ever imagined, she could not tell the two sides apart. There were robotic warriors of the same class and model on either side killing one another; none of them bore any insignia's, nor different colors or markings to tell the two factions apart except by the hail of invisible FF pings between them. Colorful plasma and ion beams of amber and blue ripped through the horde of droids. Angry red eyes glared through the smoke and darkness as ruby lasers seared their metal skin. The glittering battlefield was alive with an abstract array of destruction. These bots had turned mechanical death into a form of art.

Had the droids on this planet been battling like this for the past several decades? Ala began to wonder how many of these machines could have possibly survived that length of time, considering their violent behavior. Luckily, the two companions were fortunate enough to have been shielded from any motion sensors while hiding beneath the large broken shell where they sought shelter.

Slowly, an eerie calm fell over the smoky field as a cool breeze poured through the valley. The second setting sun glimmered for a few moments as it passed between the crest of Thebes to dip below the distant horizon. Ala and BoB dared to take a peek from behind their protective cover once they felt it was safe to move. On either side, the survivors were limping their way back towards their separate bases. There were a few who struggled, as sparks and flames spewed out of their broken shells. Those with shattered or missing limbs crawled and struggled as best they could.

Now a new plague washed onto the field. Hundreds of small beetles swarmed through the carnage, picking up whatever bits of scrap metal they could carry. Several cooperated in smalls teams to aide in dragging away pieces of larger debris. The horde of metal bugs came from either side as the weapons fire and offensive combat came to an end. It appeared like a deranged free-for-all contest to see which team of miniature drones could salvage the most parts. With surprising speed, the burned battlefield was being cleared of everything that could possibly be recycled. There were several localized incidents where scavengers from different factions would try to secure the same scrap parts, which would ensue into a brief tug of war until one side slipped in its grasp and the other sped off with its prize.

The wounded bots that were damaged and immobile, were either rescued by their dwarfish comrades or dragged away by their foes to be reprogrammed. Several of the small drones conjoined around the huge shell plate the girl had taken refuge beneath, and slowly dragged it away into the night. Ala had been deeply disturbed by what she had seen, for it was the first war she had ever witnessed and the horror of it left her in a state of shock. BoB quickly made his way towards the edge of the valley with his human companion following behind.

"What made them stop? I mean, it didn't seem like either side won," Ala questioned from behind, trying to watch her footing in the encroaching darkness.

"I must take the time to shut down and diagnose the data spool that was installed my casing if I am to fully answer that question, Ala; but it appears as if they make territorial claims in this sector by advancing forward, much like pieces on a chessboard," BoB aligned with the analogy, "Now one side will have more resource material than the other, and that calculation will depend on which side lost the most pawns." That led her to wonder how long this psychotic game had been played.

"Has this war been raging for the past three decades?" Ala asked with a wave of her hands towards the ravaged battlefield as it was being cleaned of all usable litter by the mob of scavenger drones.

"From what I have cross-referenced thus far from my memory banks, the simple answer to your question is, No," the bot replied.

Ala held her tongue; realizing BoB had been whining

about needing time to decrypt his new systems for much of the day. The edge of the valley emptied out into several shallow gullies, each one stretching towards the colony base. BoB stopped for a moment in reflection and spun back to face the girl as she caught up to him.

"Ala, there is something I need you to do," the spider asked while the girl just gave a shrug of her shoulders in reply, as she was entirely exhausted and her head was still reeling from the day's events, "The automated friend or foe transmitter in my shell almost got us killed back there," BoB admitted solemnly, and she realized he was right, "As we are approaching hostile territory, it would only be prudent that you should attempt to deactivate my FF transceiver," he advised.

"You want me to do it?" Ala responded with a boggled glance at the dented droid.

"Yes, if you could. The transmitter is hardwired into this body; I cannot simply *switch it off*," BoB confessed as he popped open a panel near the top of his dome. "There is a set of wires inside to dig through, where you should find a thin control board. There is no way to pull it out, so you must break it in order to remove it."

"Is that wise thing to do; I mean, what if we run into the bots from your side?" Ala had to ask while she made her way up the side of his dome, holding on to his leg to balance herself. It was pitch dark within the exposed compartment except for a few dim blinking lights.

"That is an unlikely event considering our current destination," he responded quickly. Ala felt around as she blindly pressed her hand through the bundle of wires within. She could tell they were attached to his antenna array, "There are two circuitry chips within, you will want to…" BoB advised before he heard a loud *SNAP!*

"Was that it?" Ala asked as she pulled out the cracked half of a circuitry board. The droid only gave a short sigh in response.

"…As I was about to say; you will want to break off the *smaller* of the two panels you find in there," the bot continued, "that was the wrong one," he finished.

"Oops," Ala gritted her teeth with a fake smile in apology. Dropping the circuit board to the sand, she dug her hand back into the small compartment to complete the task. After breaking off the remaining chip, the droid closed the compartment lid, but Ala noticed him struggling to deploy his antenna, "So, what did I break?" she asked timidly.

"You managed to get my FF identification transceiver disengaged; however, now my motion sensors seem to be offline," BoB confessed with a pale hint of despair. With a guilty shrug of her shoulders, Ala patted the droid on his shell and they continued towards the spires; looking for a safe place to spend the night and get some rest.

*   *   *

Far behind them on the edge of the valley, a single droid made its way over the crest and down into the scattered remnants of the battlefield. As it made its way through the smoking wreckage, the thinning swarm of scavenger drones continued to work; each carrying debris back to their designated base. One curious bug skittered up to the strange humanoid bot, poising its tiny red eyes as it sent a failed FF signal while trying to determine what faction the injured two-legged droid belonged to. With a surprised squeak of agony, sparks showered out as a savage slash ripped open its shell from the deep cut of a long sharpened scythe.

Controllers

From the moment he lost use of his motion sensors, BoB became ever more disoriented. When he explained to Ala how the visual optics worked in these droids, she finally understood why they had so many different eyes. Much like the inner ear is utilized in conjunction with vision for humans to keep their balance and sense of direction, such abilities were not so simple to duplicate in a machine. With their current level of technology, digital simulators created internal gyroscopes and different types of lenses were needed to analyze light and distance and all of the various spectrums in between.

Each model was equipped with an array of specialty optics that could detect heat, adapted for night vision, or even recording images. She finally had to admit their sensory array was much more complicated than she had first imagined. She was aware the use of artificial intelligence was commonplace, much like the one on her own ship; but she sure as hell didn't know how to build one nor even the basic fundamentals of how they were programmed to think on their own. Ala was familiar with plasma blasters, but they were simple in design compared to even the most generic of robots.

If it weren't for the distant dark spires of the central complex to use as a landmark they would have been wandering blind. The brooding structure remained unlit, as the bots did not require artificial lighting for their needs. Once they arrived at the outer boundary to the complex, Ala wanted to take a chance to sneak inside when she spotted something that looked like a control tower.   She assumed there would be communications equipment inside that she could utilize. If she could call her ship to come get them without having to roam the desert for the next few days, all the dandier; and this was a chance she didn't want to pass up.

BoB tried to warn her again of the risks but it was like talking to a brick wall.   When Ala's mind was set on something she was not easily swayed. Arguing that she didn't see anything moving near the tower was a weak verbal defense, but she was trying not to let BoB feel helpless in that respect, since she was the one who had accidentally damaged his circuitry.

"Look, just give me 30 minutes to call my ship; if I can't get it working we'll do things your way," Ala argued back while they both gazed upon the tall communications tower perched over the edge of the landing bay. This had clearly been the main unloading area for cargo ships, whether they were atmospheric or space-worthy vessels. The young pilot did wonder to herself, that if there was such a tight demand on resources, then why would these bots waste so much energy in volatile excursions such as the battle they had just witnessed?   BoB had to enlighten her on the extended use of solar power that the bots used to charge their battery cores; and with two suns lighting up the sky as their inexhaustible source, they had plenty of renewable energy to spare.

It was the special alloys the bots were made of that was of most value to them, along with their internal power cores which could be removed and reused without degrading their efficiency. In most cases, damaged cores could be easily repaired; they just didn't have the faculties to fabricate their own from scratch.   Ala understood that perspective, as her own ship, the Valkyrie, was a patchwork of half-assed repairs she had pieced together on her own over the years. Hell, even the ship's commode didn't function properly because she couldn't afford to install a new one; and that's not the kind of thing you could throw together with a welder.

With a measure of stealth, she leapt up onto the tarmac and scurried over to the entry doors at the base of the tower while under her companion's watchful eye. The tower was connected to the main building with a long stripe painted along its side marking a reverse silhouette of the REVO corporate logo. The wind swept through her pale mesh shawl, catching its fine material, which fluttered in the light breeze as she crossed the open deck. The soft glow of Thebes cast sparkles of light across her skin, glinting from the day's sweat. The wide tarmac of the landing platform stretched out into the distance beyond the cargo bay, lined by a row of slender antenna rods reaching up towards the shimmering stars above.

The main facility was colossal, built to accommodate the needs of several thousand colonists. The spires of the massive terraformer loomed behind it like a dark specter, overshadowing the entire complex. For now, it was deathly quiet and she was hoping it would stay that way until dawn. Ala was a tad surprised when she reached the hatch and the doors opened automatically for her when she started to jimmy the panel. Clearly, the exterior lights had been extinguished, yet there was still power running through this facility.

Ala had run salvage jobs on many failed colonies, but never on one near this scale. Terraforming projects came in all flavors, but this one had been thought out with a bigger picture in mind. By the way this place was built it was obviously well funded and used a good measure of quality engineering to meet such high standards. The REVO Corp must have been based on Earth or one of the outlying systems, Ala reasoned. They should have come back to salvage all this valuable scrap decades ago.

The interior of the lower deck had an open mess hall full of offices. Several computer units had been pulled from the walls, which looked to be the work of those little scavenger drones. That didn't give Ala much hope, especially if everything in the station had been chopped up for parts. Since she had come this far, it was worth taking a look at the upper deck of the control room. With a sigh, Ala tiptoed through the chunks of debris to a spiral stairwell near the wall; only to give a slight jump when she passed out of sensory range of the entry panel, which caused the door to slam shut behind her, leaving her in total darkness.

By hand, she blindly felt her way over to the railing, and climbed her way up the stairs. Unfortunately, the 2nd level was also void of any windows; likely designed that way to protect the building's occupants from the thrust exhaust of landing starships. She knew there was an attached hall on this level that led to the outer tower. Ala carefully edged her way along the wall into the enveloping blackness, trying to find the entry to the conjoined corridor. It was difficult to move in total darkness, and Ala almost wished she had taken up Fixer on his offer for an optical upgrade. Finding what she had believed was the door frame; she couldn't figure out how to get it open, as she was hoping it would be automated.

"Aw, crap!" she whispered aloud, while gripping the gun in her left hand. The faint glow of the pulsating energy from the tube on her implant was far too weak to see by, so she resorted to her last option. Pointing the pulse gun towards what she hoped was the far wall, Ala let off a short blast so that she could use the resulting flash to get her bearings. The energy weapon left a funnel of smoke on the wall, but before the strobe of light dissipated, she caught a glimpse of the location of the door panel and something crumpled beside it.

She realized firing off repetitive blasts would likely draw unwanted attention from any bots present inside the complex, but she had to dare one more shot so she could see what was blocking the panel. Positioning herself in front of the door, she let another shot fire; catching the split-second flash from the muzzle to handle the dust-covered lump that was leaning there. Pulling it back with her free hand just as she fired, Ala nearly fell over as she dropped the shoulder of the dry corpse she had yanked from the wall. She hadn't recognized its outline because of the layers of dust covering the carcass, and the fact that it was missing its head.

She caught a glimpse of the chain around its severed neck and the outline of an access key resting upon its chest; a small rectangular chip of plastic embedded with a digital signature in the form of tiny pins. She felt for the chain and lifted the key off the headless stump of the cadaver and fit the chip into the hole in the panel, which was a challenge to do in the dark, but she finally gave a grateful sigh as it clicked into the slot.

To her relief, the panel was powered and the door slid open to the access tunnel into the tower. Dim lights blinked on along the rim of the floor. At the end of the short hall was the locked hatch to the communications room; Ala could tell by the long gash that scarred the reinforced hatch that a Reaper had once tried to force its way inside. She wiped off the dust from the key chip and inserted it into the panel lock on the wall; with a grind, the door could only manage to slide halfway open before it jammed on the thickly scarred metal. As she expected, she found a body within; although this one had managed to retain its own head.

The tower room was actually quite small, a thin oblong deck of radar and docking system panels lined the U-shaped board. The room lit up when she entered, and she picked up the console chair that was lying on the floor to sit on. At least this room had been sealed and was relatively free of dust, except for the dried remnants of the dead pioneer. Ala struggled to get the control board to work while realizing this was decades-old technology, and was actually far more complicated to operate.

The windows overlooked the three sides of the landing port, and Ala peered out the pane to the area where BoB was supposedly hiding; although she couldn't see him. She turned on the communications board and tried to see what she could get to function. With reluctance, a vid-screen popped up from the panel and lit up; though it displayed nothing but static. Ala was getting annoyed with the befuddled arrangement of the controls as she tried to get the antennas online. Finally, with the flick of a switch, she activated the outlying towers, each blinking on as multiple red beacons lit on the tip of each tall mast.

To her shock, one after the other, the antenna towers lining the entire landing strip lit up for many miles into the distance. Ala knew she had made a serious mistake on a grand scale, since her accidentally activating the runway lights would not go unnoticed. She quickly managed to bring up a laced diagram of the complex, but couldn't get the transmitter online. Perhaps that storm had irreparably burned out the communications board, as she had half expected.

"Fuck, fuck, fuck…" Ala mumbled out loud as she tried to adjust the receptors; finally slapping her hands down on the board in aggravation, realizing she wasn't going to be able to call her ship. As she jarred the control board, a video popped onto the large monitor in front of her. It showed the dead colonist, who was now lying at her feet, and it was clear it had been recorded in that very room. The dark-haired man was in his mid 40's and appeared distraught as he spoke.

"My name is Aaron Stryker; I'm a hydrotech engineer from section 14 on the southern hub of the Avalon project, which is sponsored by the REVO Corporation. If I have uploaded this right, you should be receiving this message from the location buoy orbiting this moon," the man advised as sweat glistened upon his worried face; for it was daylight at the time of its recording. Ala knew the buoy was absent of this data log, which made it clear that there had apparently been a failure in the transmission feed to the orbital, "Several weeks ago, the colony was hit by a severe atmospheric electrical storm that blotted out communications with the outer hubs; the magnitude of the storm was so intense that we attempted to evacuate the outlying outposts. We are not sure how many survivors made it off-planet since there was a complete black-out of our receivers, so we kept trying to transmit an SOS; but so far there has been no reply to our hails," the man looked away for a moment before the log ended.

Just as quickly, a new log came back on, this one was clearly made at night, though the lights in the control room had been turned low for some reason.

"This is an update," Aaron continued, but it was hard to read his expression in the darkness of the screen, "...the last time I saw the base commander he had ordered our few remaining airships be sent out to search for survivors. It is now clear that the storm has knocked out the transmitters with something that resembled the effects of an electromagnetic pulse. We have very few personnel left here, and we don't know how many escaped during the squall ...or why they have not come back to rescue us. I got stuck here at the main facility while retrieving essential cargo, but none of the ground transports are functional either. Everything that was exposed to the storm front seems to have been disabled, all except for the worker droids here, which must have been shielded somehow," he added, but Ala noted a sound of disbelief in his voice, "Some of them have gone haywire, and been observed acting outside of their original programming," Stryker's entry abruptly ended, only to continue with yet another new log; in this one it appeared to have been recorded during the early morning, as the dim purple sky in the background glimmered with color.

"New log; it's been a few days now, most of the personnel that were here recently left to check on their families on the outer rim since none of the scout ships have returned. There are only two dozen or so people left in the complex, as we thought it best to wait here for a rescue ship." Aaron added with a troubled stutter, he continued, "Several of the droids in storage have self-activated. Yesterday we sent a crew down to resolve the situation but they haven't reported back in. There seems to be a flaw in the robotic programming, but we have no way to deactivate them as all the repair stations are down," Stryker noted as the screen cut to the outside camera of the tarmac below, showing a mass of worker bots milling about the landing area. After a few minutes, the recording changed again. It was still dim outside in the video, however, this time the engineer seemed to be on the edge of hysteria. There was a woman in a white jumpsuit sitting in the background; Ala recognized the access key hanging around her neck.

"It has been several weeks since the others went to find the missing colonists, there are only nine of us left here at the control complex. Renee, here, is a droid tech who was working on the drilling platform for Outpost 21," Stryker added as he scooted over while the woman moved into view of the camera, "I was present when the well level at Station 21 suddenly dropped, causing the sumps to collapsed. There seemed to be no seismic activity, but for some reason the water table in that sector plunged to undetectable levels; shortly thereafter, stations 1 thru 20 on the outlying hubs also reported the same readings," Renee reported as she turned to Aaron who whispered a few words to her off screen. Continuing with her report, she seemed a little frazzled about something, "We were preparing to bring the hydropower plant online to start processing the drawn water we had tapped from the aquifers when the devastating surface storm we had experienced began to develop. I don't believe it was a simple coincidence," Renee turned as she began to squabble about certain engineering details with Stryker. Then the log abruptly cut off.

The log record went black for a long spell, and Ala was about to reach over to switch it off when another recording popped back on. It was Aaron again.

"Against my better judgment, I deleted Renee's last log

entry for professional reasons, since her eccentric views would risk getting her dismissed from the project if the corporate executives got wind of the absurd theories she's been trying to feed the rest of the staff. There are only four of us left now; myself, Tyler, Renee, and Milan; we found Connors immolated body down in the storage bay hours ago, likely caused by a malfunction in the plasma conduits he was near. We don't know where the others went," Stryker added with a despairing glance out the window to his right. "Tyler said he saw a bot that wasn't on the design charts roaming about on the docking platform. We didn't believe him until we recently observed several more of them crossing the tarmac from the direction of the loading bay; they seemed to be carrying some type of machete. There is no application or use for any of our worker droids to have such an accessory," the weary engineer conceded.

From the log dates it seemed that the recorded events had spanned over several weeks since the freak storm had struck the facility. With their numbers being whittled down and the lack of any communication coming from the emptiness of space, these few survivors were being psychologically strained to the edge; trying to make sense of what had happened while awaiting a rescue that would never come. There was one last entry that grabbed Ala's attention. Aaron came back on the screen, it was dark outside again in the recording; Stryker had turned all the lights off in the communications room, only the dim controls from the panel blinked coldly in the background.

"The droids have gone berserk; we saw many of them trying to break into the complex by force. Luckily, most of them are too large to make it into the upper levels of the personnel station, but…" Aaron trailed off as he looked out the window into the darkness, "I …I don't recognize any of these robotic models," the camera view switched once again out onto the tarmac that the control tower overlooked. Like crimson candles, the glowing red eyes from hundreds of remodeled and deformed constructs crept across the landing platform. After a few seconds, the engineer came back on the screen; clearly dehydrated and upset to the point of being incoherent.

"I've had to seal the door to the control room; nobody else is answering the intercom. I don't think anyone is coming for us…" The end of the transmission went to static and then blinked off a final time.

Ala sat there in silence; it was a lot to take in. She hadn't been keeping a close track of time, but BoB would be expecting her in short order. With a last check on the diagram of the complex, she switched off the panel and sat back in the chair for a second in hesitation; then reached out and turned the screen back on and activated the data file to record her statement.

"This is the captain of the Valkyrie, and I am recording this sub-log thirty years after the demise of this colony and its personnel, in the event that I don't make it off this forsaken rock," Ala stated while trying to hold back the lump in her throat, with the reality of what she had learned over the past several days sinking in. She had never felt so entirely alone in her life as she did sitting in that communications room chair, suddenly filled with self-doubt, "The colony's worker droids are the only survivors left on this planet; and have somehow evolved to a dangerously hostile level. I was separated from my ship and am now making my way back to outpost station zero-niner. If anyone should find this message log, I would advise that you leave this sector immediately and avoid all contact with the native bots roaming the surface, nor make any attempt to salvage this facility; lest you become stranded here yourselves," Ala finished, but then chose to add one last tidbit to the log before signing off, "The Avalon project was a failure; I don't know what it is, but there is something else at hand here that I can't explain. From what I've seen, I can't help but feel that Tranquility is a place where our species doesn't belong."

It was a solemn note to end on, but she felt there was a tone of credibility to her statements. Turning off the control panel, Ala squeezed out the hatch and jammed the hall door open so she could use the residual light to find her way to the stairwell. The ground floor was still enveloped in darkness, but she knew where the doorway was. While making her way through the shadows to the location of the panel, something fell to the floor with a crash behind her; she spun around to see an array of tiny red glowing eyes peering at her from behind a doorway. As the portal exit opened, she could tell by its outline it was a scavenger drone, similar to the small bots she had seen swarming the battlefield after the conflict.

The little bot stared at her for a few seconds as their eyes locked, and then it quickly turned about and skittered off into the darkness. Ala took that as her cue to leave, as likely the little tattletale would report her presence to the other bots in the complex. She didn't relish the thought of being captured again by either faction of droids, so she hurried off across the tarmac to where she had left BoB. As she jumped back down into the shadow of the platform; she found her companion had disappeared. Now she was worried.

"Bob …Bob! Goddammit; where the hell are you?" Ala

whispered as loud as she dared, searching the edge of the platform wall in vain. Tracing her way through the sand towards the interior hub, she saw a ramp leading to the upper deck. Figuring BoB had come searching for her; she thought it was worth taking a peek inside. She looked around to see if she could find any of his unique footprints in the sand, but it was far too dark to make out such details. Ala cautiously made her way to the edge of the ramp and proceeded up the steep slope by the bright starlight overhead.

She spotted a wide-open door that he might fit into at the far corner of the personnel station and took a few steps toward the opening. With a turn of her foot, she took cover behind a supporting beam just as several rogue droids skittered across the landing platform towards the communications tower; their glowing red eyes lighting up the area as they passed. Ala froze as one bot stopped to take a sensor scan in her direction; after not detecting any movement, it turned and followed its comrades.

If BoB was in there, he was as good as spare parts; Ala sighed to herself. She didn't like getting separated; but this little excursion had been her foolish idea in the first place, so she had no one else to blame. She decided to make her way back to where she had left BoB and wait for him there, but that course of action was cut short when one of the robotic sentries pranced out to the very edge of the platform wall and stationed itself there. Cursing to herself, Ala made her way through the support pillars of the colossal terraformer as she remembered what she could from the diagram up in the control tower.

Sneaking her way through the corridors, Ala spotted several droids coalesced into small groups. Many were damaged survivors from the recent battle being refitted and repaired. Discovering a pedestrian walkway, she quietly made her way up the narrow stair to the upper level; appreciating for the first time how stealthy and silent she could be on her bare feet. Far below, she passed over showers of glowing sparks as tech bots were busy at work repairing their wounded soldiers. She could see several of the small scavenger drones separating scrap metal from one pile to the next.

Ala knew she had wandered into the wasp's nest. If she got caught here, there would be no escape. Luckily, there were still many areas that these large robots could not access, such as the thin walkway she was crossing. Ala realized that if she couldn't find BoB, then she would be hard up for food and water on the long trek ahead. She was aware of the direction she needed to head in, but it was still a great way off and would be suffering by the end of it if she made a go at it alone. Maybe her companion had already been captured and he was being dismantled somewhere below? That horrid thought crossed her mind as quickly as she tried to dismiss it.

The terraformer itself was a massive structure, with several sub-chambers and vaulted levels for processing the air. There was also a central collector that vacuumed and filtered gasses in the atmosphere, remixing it at a molecular level to make it more Earth-norm. From the ceiling, the tall spires funneled massive power conduits that fed from the exterior shell that were lined with solar panels. The entire skin was covered in micro-cells that converted the daylight into usable energy. This was the ageless power source the bots had relied upon for their survival. The energy collected was stored within a hoard of battery cores they had lined like clutches of eggs around the capacitor towers. The batteries could absorb the converted electrical energy and recharge the cores without needing to be directly connected; several bots were poised around these to draw energy themselves.

She started to head into a dark corner for cover; then remembered she was foolishly thinking with her human eyes in mind. With their electronic optics, these bots could likely see into the infrared range and wavelengths that no dark shadow could hide; she would have to keep clear out of sight. Ala stepped down to the ground floor and froze when one of the oversized droids shifted its multiple legs. With their glowing red eyes shut off, she realized they had powered down to recharge.

A portal door hissed open as she approached the darkened wall, and Ala slipped into the corridor beyond. The access tunnel twisted like a snake through the complex, hiding doorways beyond every curve. The young girl made her way to an adjacent tunnel and continued to cling to the wall of the corridor. As this structure was open to the sky, it would be far easier to see where she was going when dawn arrived; though she planned on being long gone before then.

With a *tap, tap, tap,* of metal; Ala heard a bot approach. Slipping around the archway to escape it, the damn robot kept approaching her direction. As quickly as she could, Ala ran for a side corridor and dived into an empty storage room; quietly closing the door behind her. Listening, she could hear the pursuing bot get closer then suddenly stopping at the door. Trying to hold her breath and keeping silent, for a frightening moment she wondered if the droid's sensors were sensitive enough to hear her heartbeat. With a startle, the door slid open; and there was nowhere for Ala to hide.

Michel Savage

Voices Within

A large robot with several red eyes glared at her from the doorway.

"Ala, it's me, Bah-b," her companion whispered. The girl had almost fainted out of fright, responding with a loud sigh as she let herself breathe. BoB scrunched his legs together and was just barely able to wiggle his bulk through the double-wide door.

"Where the hell did you go …and how did you find me?" the girl inquired with an accusing glare, entirely forgetting about her tracer implant Fixer had installed within her armband.

"Since your translator only works at close range, I had asked Fixer to implant a tracking…"

"Oh shit, that's right; it had slipped my mind," Ala interrupted, "…but why the hell did you leave me out there alone?" She demanded.

"My apologies, Ala; I knew you were up in the tower, but I heard something coming from this building …and since you had broken my motion sensor, I thought it would be prudent to take a moment to investigate since you had not moved from the flight tower for quite some time," BoB responded back, clearing the air, "I was returning to our rendezvous point when I noticed your proximity via your implant. Thus, I followed you here," the spider bot paused as he spun his dome around, scanning the small room in confusion, "May I question as to why this particular chamber was your destination?" He added in a wry tone.

"I thought you were one of them…" Ala sighed.

"But …*I am* one of them. That observation does not explain why you came to this chamber," BoB retorted bluntly, not quite following her faulty logic.

"No, I meant one of *them* …as in one of the other bots, I don't have one of those identity ping zapper gizmos like you do …or did," she complained, catching her mistake at the last second with a guilty smirk. Reflecting on that detail, the girl recalled that her implant could sense the presence of the FF pings, but she hadn't noticed any since they entered this base. She informed BoB of that fact and he advised her that they were not necessary within each faction's home ground. Any approaching foes would have already been detected should they encroached upon the outer perimeter, but he hadn't been spotted since she had disabled the device BoB had inside his new body.

Sitting down for a moment, Ala reflected on what the bot had just said. He looked funny there, with his legs all bunched up in the small room.

"You said you heard something …like what?" she asked with a quizzical tilt of her head.

"I can still hear them now, can't you?" He responded with a nervous shift of his dome.

"Them ...them who?" Ala asked with a scrunched brow as she put her ear to the door.

"The voices," BoB confessed, "Your digital receptor is very weak, but perhaps if you got closer to the source…" he trailed off, never finishing his sentence.

The young girl thought it was worth a look to inspect this electronic noise the droid had sensed; not only to satisfy her own curiosity but to fill any explanation for the mystery that had been unfolding here since she had arrived. She reflected on all of the unfortunate settlers who had disappeared or died, and it was as if the entire galaxy had never noticed. With a sad thought, Ala realized that if she met her end out here somewhere in deep space, it was quite likely that nobody would remember her either. But then, she knew she was just a nobody; a lowlife scavy no one would really miss, but there had been several thousand people here with real lives and families. After all this time, someone had to start asking questions on their behalf.

Peeking her head out the doorway, they stepped out into the hall as she followed BoB through the complex towards the voices within. More than once they had to take cover from passing sentries, but finally arrived at the central chamber. A ringed platform with open rails sat perched at its center. Large mechanical drills lined the walls while cargo containers were seen stacked about the room. On an upper deck, they could see several bots milling about their duties; but since none initiated any pings, BoB went unnoticed; but Ala had to hide from direct view behind his bulky shell as best she could.

"It's down there," BoB advised her in a hushed tone.

"Where?" Ala retorted, lost to where he was referring to as they were standing on the ground floor. The metal spider skittered over to the central platform rail where he pointed out a control panel with a latched joystick. She could understand how the bots would have been unable to operate the device since it was made for human hands. It took a few moments for her to figure out how to activate it, and with a push of a few buttons to power it up, she clutched the switch on the stick. They steadied themselves as the floor gave a sudden shudder. With a grinding of gears, the round platform began to sink, dropping them into a deep chamber below.

There were scored edges among the rock, but for the most part the ground below the station showed signs of natural weathering. Ala realized the settlers had built this massive terraformer directly over a natural cavern, while the platform sunk lower into the darkness below. With a grinding whir, the lift came to a halt with a puff of dust as they reached the bottom. Proximity lights blinked on around the large underground grotto. There was old machinery here and a bank of computers hardwired to the station above; thick cables lined the rock walls, snaking their way across the coarse stone to the ceiling high above them.

A chill permeated the room as a thin fog floated across the slick stone floor; accenting the stillness of the cavern. All the surrounding equipment was covered with layers of fine dust; it was evident that the bots had never accessed this level before. In the dead silence underground, her senses began to tingle. In a far corner lay a row of control desks and monitors covered with a thick film of dirt. Drilling pipes were stacked on the opposite end of the room along with several storage tanks. There was a great deal of scientific paraphernalia and other odds and ends she didn't recognize, but it was the control desks that seemed to have been wired to draw the most power.

The panels sat in a semicircle around a large black ring embedded into the rock floor. Taking a closer look, Ala took a wary step back as she realized the abysmal blackness in its center was actually a gaping hole. The cranes and machinery poised above it seemed to be used for lowering devices into its murky depths. When she approached it, she could tell what BoB had been talking about all this time. Resonating through her bones, the digital receptor in her implant picked up on the electronic noise. They sounded like whispers; hundreds, then thousands of them growing louder by the moment, uttering something unintelligible.

"Do you hear them now, Ala?" BoB asked, as he walked about inspecting the room on his stalks, finally coming to rest at her side.

"Yes …what is that?" Ala wondered, a little troubled by the rising chatter. She instinctively put her hands to her ears for a moment to block out the noise, until she realized it didn't help in the slightest as the sound was being received through her implant. These voices weren't audible to the human ear, only the robots could hear them. They seemed to be coming from the dark shaft. Ala was a little more than disturbed by this.

Making her way over to the console, she brushed away the layers of dust that had caked the screens and control panels. With the twist of a switch, the panel lit up as power surged through the idle system. Ala was determined to find out what the hell was going on down here. For lack of chairs, she found a small crate to sit upon while she fiddled with the board; trying to make sense of the old equipment. The diagram displayed there showed the projected timeline for the terraforming process, and Ala brought up the horizontal file tree that the REVO enterprise was so fond of using.

The 1st through 2nd cycles were meant to establish the foundations of the main base, and a great majority of building fabrication was assisted by construction bots who erected the primary command post facilities. It wasn't until the 3rd cycle that the colonists were able to go outside without respirators for limited time spans. A full soil analysis of the location was then processed and diagramed. Jumping to the end of the 6th cycle, they ceased building hydroponics greenhouses as they had planned a transitioning stage that would start altering soil composition of the lunar environment.

They introduced specific chemical and mineral changes by a washboard effect; taking the moisture they began pumping water from the aquifers deep below the surface and spraying the diluted mineral mixture onto the topsoil. This process would take a full decade to complete; but their primary analysis of its effects would only take a fraction of that time. There were various notes logged within that reported this process had never been attempted on such a grand scale, and after several cycles of monitoring their progress they had finally began to see positive results. The colonists had been successful at altering the moon's native soil to be able to support Terran plant life.

Ala gave a curious sigh as she read through the tabs in the extensive log. It appeared that the Avalon project had been going pretty near to plan until the end of the decade. With 2/3rds of the process complete, the stubborn engineers weren't about to let anything stand in their way; even incidental mishaps. There were two dozen pumping stations listed on the master chart to be built, all aligned in a circumference far outside the main facility; much like spokes on a wheel. When the majority of them came online, they began pumping the underground water reservoirs at high capacity once the first test phase showed the ability to nurture native Terran plants.

This was a boon for the scientists and engineers on the project, as they were proving there was no need to force genetic changes into their vegetation to make it compatible with any given alien soil, but they could instead attack the problem visa-versa. A century before, during the first colonization of Mars, several experimental attempts at growing food in Martian soil turned out to be problematic at best. They came up with meager results after balancing the PH levels and introduction of essential minerals in an effort to make the soil more user friendly with the foreign test plants.

Such trials were repeated on several alien worlds, but the native Earth plants mutated in ways that drastically altered their taste and composition; along with changing in size and color. However, the most troubling part was that nearly every type of vegetation they introduced into the alien soil ended up modified in unpredictable ways. Tomato plants ended up seedless, as did many other types of Terran plants that became completely unrecognizable. As a result of that failed endeavor, colonists had to rely heavily on the artificial gel commonly used as a replacement for soil in hydroponics gardens. Because of that single failure, all water that was processed for the plants had to be injected with special nutrients the plants needed; which made its use and even runoff unfit for human consumption without inserting several levels of exceptionally complicated and very expensive filtering processes to make the recycling system work.

The problem was that greenhouses themselves were in fact a major burden to all colonization projects. Expensive domes and protective shelters that could have been used for habitats were allocated for plants and specialized botanists, taking up a great deal of valuable space and attention; but were necessary for both food and oxygen production. The massive terraformer was used to change the composition of the atmosphere itself, which would positively change the temperature and UV radiation to acceptable levels for any exterior growing plant life; without all the need for shielding or solar filters. Thus, forcing the alien soil of any given off world colony site to synchronize with their needs would free up a great deal of time and energy for future generations.

Ala could understand that fact, as the engineers were looking for ways around the requirement for sealed habitats to garden oxygen and food production, and the need to funnel such an extensive amount of resources towards its care. So they began to think big, by changing the native soil to fit their needs. It was logged that open crop production began on the 10th cycle of their test phase. They had completed construction of the 24 pumping stations by that time and began to spray the surface with the chemical additives they had introduced into the water, aimed to filter through the strata back into the subsurface aquifers.

At the same time the atmosphere processor had also reached a critical stage, which had started to create condensation clouds in the upper stratosphere. Thus, nobody paid too much attention to the isolated electrical storms that began to form around Tranquility. The year before the cataclysmic storm had hit, they had introduced Terran insects into the environment to aid the plants with cross-pollination and to help balance the ecosystem, trying to complete the process 'the natural way' as they kept trying to tout. Ala was a bit flabbergasted when she read that they had also introduced several species of small Terran fruit bats to assist with both pollinating the plants and also to aid with any possible insect overpopulation as a control predator. Ala recalled the sheer size of the monstrous bat that had attacked them, compared to the sample images displayed on the screen in front of her. Obviously, some disturbing mutations had directly afflicted them over the past several decades.

The completion bar on the data tree ended at cycle 12; when all this shit started to go topsy-turvy on them. The real question was; what the hell was this dark pit lying in front of her? The computer AI built into the station seemed to be malfunctioning in a way she had never seen before. It wasn't just static or garble that was spewing out, but strange poetic garbage that didn't make any sense. It was obviously online, but fragmented in ways that were hard to fathom. BoB was just as confounded, so he made a suggestion.

"Ala, this model droid they built me into does in fact have a hardwire port," He advised her, "it's what they use to reprogram new robots through a laced interface, like the one I have."

"What good would that do?" Ala inquired, as her frustration began to simmer, "Listen to it, the system's core is completely fucked," she added, as the computer babbled on insistently without pause. It spoke lines of words endlessly, strung together without meaning or pause. The computer itself was non-responsive; Ala figured its vital circuits must have gotten fried during that freak storm ages ago, which had knocked out most everything else on the planet.

"I could attempt to translate what it is saying. I note that there is a repeating sequence in the pattern, so it might help if I were to be plugged directly into it," he suggested.

"But, it's not saying *anything*," she shrugged, giving the screen a glance of mild annoyance, "it's just blabbering nonsense."

"Actually, Ala," BoB responded, "both the computer

and the voices seem to be speaking in unison patterns, just slightly out of phase," he asserted. Ala just sat there for a long moment with a stunned look on her face; BoB shifted his dome for a second to see if there was a reason she was malfunctioning, "Did you hear me, Ala?"

"Yeah ...uh, let me find a hardwire coil," she replied while getting up to take a look around the room. She found a stash of them piled in a storage container on the platform. The cord was long enough to reach from the table and over to the dark cavity where the droid stood. In a slit below his sharp mandibles she found a standard plug into which the connector fit, since the bots had never upgraded their own core technology.

"Alright, I'm plugging you in now," She warned BoB as she slipped in the connection. Within seconds, she realized that it had probably been a mistake to do that. The thick cord hummed and fizzled as power surged through it. Ala stepped away as tiny electrical arcs escaped from BoB's exterior shell. His multiple eyes began to glow in surges and he stepped forward to the black ring, staring down over the breach and into the dark void below. The searing arcs became more intense as streams of blue electricity flashed over his body, and Ala was afraid his circuits were going to get fried. She reached out to disconnect the plug, only to pull her hand back in a yelp of pain when it burned her.

"It's alright Ala," the droid slowly turned his dome to her for a brief moment while several bright fingers of electricity danced over his body like webs of light, "I just need..." BoB stalled as his voice faded to nothing. The droids multiple eyes all dimmed into a low power state and a voice that wasn't his, spoke. She found it mentally challenging listening to the alien whispers humming through her implant along with the droning speech from the main computer. BoB spoke with the strange voice that was slightly off-key as his words echoed upon themselves, Ala found it all quite creepy.

"…There is still one, find it, destroy it," he trailed the words out slowly, "Save me; there is still one; find it, destroy it," Bob repeated, over and over.

'Still one what?' she had tried to ask him, but BoB was non-responsive, it was like something had suppressed his AI processor and had taken control of him. Desperately looking around, Ala couldn't find anything to use to insulate the wire from burning her hands so she could yank out the plug. Taking the risk of ruining her pulse gun, she swatted the connection by using its barrel, yanking the wire free but received a nasty shock in the process.

The electrical surge around the lip of the pit ceased when the wire from the console broke loose and the droid slumped to the floor. Residual static emptied into the ground around him as Ala took a few steps forward.

"Bob? Hey …are you in there?" the girl inquired as she tapped on his metallic shell while giving a nervous glance around, wondering what she should do.

Ala fell back in alarm on the dusty floor, gun in hand pointing at BoB when the droid suddenly jolted upright with its eyes glowing fiercely. She realized her little pop gun would do little against his two mounted cannons while she laid there in shock, waiting for the bot to react. With a slow whir, the spider's legs loosened to drop his shell slowly back to the floor and the glaring eyes on his dome all turned to the girl lying helpless on the ground before him.

"Ala, we need to leave," he finally said in his own voice

once again. In the background of the room she could hear the monotone jabbering of the computer and the strange whispers from the hole resume once again.

"What just happened? I thought that you were going to attack me," she confessed with a note of fear, not knowing what else to say in the awkward moment while she rose to her feet, "You asked me to save you, and you said something about there still being one, and needing to destroy it," the young scavenger stated nervously.

"I recall the words I said, Ala, but I was not asking you to save *me*; I was simply acting as the translator," he paused for a troubled moment, "I now realize that this is the entity that had reprogrammed the other robots with their new primary directives," BoB explained to her utter disbelief, "When it was making the request to *find it and destroy it* ...I'm afraid it was talking about you, Ala."

The Reaper

Ala's reality was shattered, this was insane! What kind of freaky alien bullshit was this?

"Bob, what the fuck did you mean by calling it an *entity*?" Ala demanded; it was clear she didn't like being left in the dark, "Are all these robots out to kill me now?"

"I don't believe it was speaking to the other droids in the vicinity, otherwise I would have been able to decipher the command myself without being directly plugged in," BoB admitted, "If I were to guess, it was a message encoded for a very specific class of droid unlike any we have encountered thus far," he admitted, "and I simply referred to the source of the transmissions as an *'entity'* for lack of any other logical description available."

Despite the droid's urge to leave the facility in haste, Ala tried to keep a rational grip on the situation. Sitting back down at the console again, she began flipping back through the file logs. She wanted to find out exactly what that chasm in the floor was, and where it led to. Catching something of interest, she backed up the data tree and found several entries by the robotic technician named Renee. What Ala discovered there was boggling.

Renee had made her way to this work station several times while the survivors were awaiting rescue after the storm. She had noted that Aaron Stryker had deleted many of her entries into the official transmission log, and that there was a great deal of tension between her and the rest of the remaining crew. Renee admitted she tended to be a bit outspoken among her colleagues, but had a genuine reason for her conduct at the time. In her log she provided a subtle reference to a hidden file at the end of one of her written entries; which she had specifically created to prevent from being deleted due to Stryker's attempts to silence her. She simply referenced it as file GAIA. BoB came around the control table to view the screen beside her as Ala began to play the video log.

"I have been forced to record this data on the laboratory files since one of our senior engineers has chosen to erase my formal entries," Renee spoke calmly from the video log, though she did seem a tad uncomfortable, "Despite what my associates might say about me, I am not unbalanced or delusional. I have several degrees, some of which were in studies of ancient cultures and lost civilizations of Terra Prime; which I understand is not common reading material for most colonist or even our high-level corporate executives," she humbly admitted, "I'm a specialist in robotic repairs and programming, but I began to notice some anomalies in the behavior of our worker bots recently. When I witnessed the aquifer failure that affected our pumping stations, I recalled several case studies from my early years in the field. When the violent electrical storms started to emerge across the globe of Tranquility, I couldn't keep silent any longer and decided to voice my theories to the administration …and to my humiliation, my concepts were only met with ridicule," Renee added with a disgruntled sigh.

Ala listened on as the extensive log continued, while trying to absorb every word; it was all a bit much. The tech made reference to a religious cult that died out over a century ago near the end of the bloody 4th Terran world war that had spread throughout the solar system of Earth. There had been a mass uprising of a certain devout sect that pushed their occult beliefs in the Gaia theory. These nut jobs became so affluent that they superseded every other religion that had ever been followed throughout human history. They're theology was the same old Mother Earth and revolt of nature crap that the bleeding heart conservationists kept feeding to anyone and everyone associated with the world's governments; who of course, never bothered to listen. In short, they literally believed that the Earth was a living entity, and we were killing it.

On one level, they were right; mankind certainly ass fucked the ecosystem of planet Earth right out the window. Sure, there was an extensive history of such cults from medieval times, even back to the days of the druids and long before recorded history that fueled such lunacy. But the way that Renee had explained it, a few of her summaries started to make a bit of sense, which certainly threw Ala for a curve. There were and had been multiple nature conservation movements that had sprung up to counter the amount of pollution and synthetic poison our species was drowning in. But as time would tell, it was the iron will of the financial corporations that would eventually win out; and it was that old mentality that Renee was fighting against, and she knew it.

In her lengthy debate recorded within the log, she did have a valid point about mankind having destroyed the once pristine environment of Earth; which inevitably forced us to spread out among the stars to escape the cesspool we had created of our homeworld. Still, she kept bringing up ancient historical references and making radical statements about *the Earth is a living being* bullshit; which Ala imagined would have gotten the REVO Corporate Executives pretty riled. Ala had experienced a lot of weird shit lately, so she sat there flipping through the file without a smirk or giggle as she would have likely done several weeks prior.

"The top argument I encountered was the fact that the Avalon project was not creating any pollutants on this planet that we perceived," Renee's log continued, "but fundamentally, we were in fact changing the environment in countless ultra-radical ways that the moon itself could not tolerate," She added. "I realize that the followers of the Gaia faith died out long before the beginning of the colonization of the outer cosmos, but it was the belief of their cult that our own mother Earth had been responding to mankind's damaging presence in the form of global catastrophes," she concluded, "What we thought were mere virus outbreaks and erratic climate changes as an effect of our pollution, could possibly, and I quote here, *possibly*, could have been an intentional act of retaliation by the Earth, itself."

Ala cut off the video log and read the sub-notes left below glowing on the screen. No wonder Stryker had gagged her, this loon was trying to suggest to the upper management that by altering the biosphere and chemical composition of the native lunar soil, that they were enraging the planet to revolt against them. So, that was the meat of it, the colonists were pissing off the planet itself? Ala almost laughed at Renee's expense. It wasn't the mere presence of the colonists here that had evoked the following events, which the tech was trying to outline but their actual attack on the base elements and native species already present on this world.

Ala had seen a handful of terraforming projects where the biological life disagreed with the human colonists that invaded their world, but this crazy bitch was trying to spoon-feed her colleagues that it was the planet itself, as a whole, that was irate and reacting to protect itself. Then again, they were all rotting bones in the sand now; and maybe it was Renee who got the last laugh after all. Ala remembered the headless corpse of the woman she had found lying against the door panel. She sat there brooding about the sheer irony of the technician ending up getting killed by something she helped to create.

The central file explained that this natural subterranean chamber was the first station where the original core samples had been drilled when they were choosing a location to develop, and consequently, had built the main complex over this site. With persistence, BoB finally won with his urgings for them to exit the base quickly; daylight would be coming soon, and with it a majority of the bots would awaken from stasis.

They made their way back to the lift. With the hissing of pistons, the gears of the elevator kicked in and raised the platform back to the ground floor. They could still see several technician bots on the upper levels roaming about, checking the energy towers that were feeding the power cores below. Through the domed sphere high above, Ala noticed the night sky was beginning to wane. The river of stars began to fade as the deep hue of the evening sky slowly drifted over the heavens above as it fled from the approaching dawn.

It was a tricky feat to find their way out of the complex again, as Ala had entirely blanked out on the diagram of the facility after recently drowning herself in the file logs but they eventually made their way to an exterior exit. On the far side of the complex the sands had drifted away from the outer wall, leaving a steep drop-off to either side. Painted on the floor was the faded marker to drilling station 09, a sign meant to be visible from the base control tower that led to Outpost 9. From this distance, Ala could now tell that the communications tower was designed to rotate around the central complex to each platform hub. Now, it was just a matter of time to get far enough out of sight from the droids that controlled this facility and back to her ship.

*   *   *

Back inside the complex, within the main chamber at the edge of the lift platform, were Ala and her companion had stood moments before; a single droid unique to all others, stood listening. Its large single eye pulsated with renewed energy, absorbing power from the surrounding towers. On its last active mission, it had stormed an escaping personnel shuttle full of human controllers. Its fellow comrades had fallen to the wayside as the transport ship made an emergency launch in an effort to escape the approaching horde of murderous bots, leaving the single Hellbot aboard to complete its task alone.

The G series were specifically designed for high risk indoor combat such as this. Made of a high-grade armored alloy, its shell had been pieced together from the defense system that had once been mounted on the outer walls. Its single eye had the ability to see through electronic camouflage and identify living heat signatures. It used its integrated pulse rifle to take out ranged targets whenever an armed human pointed a weapon his way; its targeting locked in and disposed of the enemy with a single round. Pulse weapons did little damage to metal and stone, but were devastating against flesh and bone.

The Reaper much preferred to use its weapon of choice, one which was entirely unique among the other bot models; a short-range flame thrower that incinerated its fragile targets. It could not understand the logic these controllers put in raising a vocal alarm; why did nearly all of them react as though it were necessary to scream? Their irrational behavior was simply beyond analysis; per its programmed instructions, it used its scythe arm to assure their complete deactivation by removing the heads of every Controller it encountered.

It recalled the transport shipped had rocked when it had taken off, making the first few dozen colonists easy prey as they stumbled over one another in the chaos. Acrid smoke of burnt clothing and flesh began to waft through the back of the ship, obstructing the view of all aboard, except for the Reaper's specialized optics.   Many floundered over one another to escape the reach of his sharp scythe, detaching limbs as he tore through their soft flesh, crippling their efforts to escape. It was all too easy. Many strapped into their launch chairs never knew what hit them; he remembered the distorted look on one humans face as it turned to him in fright before it was permanently silenced.

The majority of them made a run for the forward cabin and into the cockpit, fumbling over the pilots in their hysterics. One of the humans slammed the cabin door closed on the rest of the crew behind him, locking them in the passenger cabin with the Hellbot; an illogical move, but a tactic the bot knew well. The trapped humans screamed in alarm so loudly that he wished nothing more than to cease their endless wailing. Several of them made a move to jump him, finally showing a degree of bravery in the very end. A spurt of flame and they would crumble; releasing him from their withered grasp as their skin melted and burned.

The robots external microphones picked up additional

screams from the humans on the other side of the locked hatch to the cockpit just as several shots rang out. The entire ship suddenly lurched and dived to the ground. There was the violent jolt of an impact and everyone and everything went blissfully silent. He was buried under the weight of their bodies. For all the red liquid and soft flesh they were made of, these humans were heavy, and he found he could not move. There was no use in stressing his vital gears, for the Reaper was confident his robotic comrades would soon find and free him; so he initiated his shutdown sequence to conserve power.

Everything was black and silent for a very, very long time. His reserve power was so low he almost didn't come out of stasis. His microphones were compacted with dust, but he had heard a familiar noise after his motion sensors initiated. For some reason his gears were jammed, at first activation they almost failed to budge. It was a human voice that had awoken him; his mission was incomplete. He found that the corpses of the controllers piled upon him were much lighter to move now, though failing to understanding the process of decay on organic tissue. One of his knees and multiple sections of its ankle joints were bent, but he managed to exit the ship by a side port hatch which had been left ajar.

By the tracks, he could tell a bot had been there recently, which he assumed, had freed the access door for him to escape. He needed to make his way back to the main base, but first he required a few hours to replenish his severely depleted energy cells with the solar chips embedded on the back of his armored hood. The forgotten Reaper stood there in the fading daylight like a statue of death, raised from the grave after decades of quiet slumber. It had not realized the length of time that had passed, for it had no internal clock programmed into its data core; these robotic slayers had no need for them.

After sunset, it shut down its trickle charger, as it now had barely enough energy to make its trek back to the base station. Upon running initial diagnostics, the bot noted its internal tank of flammable liquid fuel had evaporated. Its pulse gun was still functional but only at minimal level and would need to be recharged, and its top movement speed had been crippled during the impact of the wrecked transport ship. As it made its way through the darkness, it noted the flares of a distant battle at hand; presuming these pathetic human controllers might have put up a final resistance after all.

During the time his model was built, there were no separate factions. Hellbot's had been programmed with one single instruction; to protect this moon from invasion and that their human controllers must be eradicated to that end. As he encroached upon the battlefield, the Reaper noted no presumed human casualties, only strange robots that fired undecipherable digital pings towards him. He took offense at that, as the small drones seemed to be little more than nuisances without purpose. The base was much farther away than he remembered, and the landscape somewhat different than previously recorded; but it was of no consequence.

He was one of the first altered combat droids whom were constructed without any FF programming or faction designation.   The Hellbot was beyond neutrality, he walked among them digitally invisible. The proximity of the energy towers fully replenished his depleted power cells. The repair technician droids here looked different and failed to make any response to repair his limbs upon his repeated commands.   His retired model had been decommissioned after the demise of the colonists; to them, he was nothing more than a walking ghost. The G series android reported to the central chamber; although now the area was modified and littered with debris, and surmised that his memory chip might have been fractured in the recent crash he had suffered. The plea from a familiar voice spoke to him from the abyss below.

"*I will save you; I will find it, I will destroy it*," the Reaper assured the bodiless entity, and turned to follow the thermal trail Ala had left in her wake. Her warm footprints were easy enough to follow as it filtered the heat signatures of her every step leading to the exit beyond the walls.

*　*　*

Outside, Ala and her spider droid made their way across the hub wall towards station nine. After all the grief she had been through to get here, the young pilot was eager to get back to the safety of her ship. In quiet thought, she pondered whether to take BoB with her when she finally jetted off this rock; she figured the unique model droid might be worth a decent handful of credits to some collector, but placing a fully armed robot in the storage hold that could blow a hole out of her ship on a whim, was a bit of a risk. What if he decided to malfunction in the middle of a light jump? There were just too many variables to consider; Ala figured it was a decision she would have to make when she crossed that bridge.

The path ahead stretched far out into the horizon. With a shrug, Ala reckoned it would take at least another day on foot to reach the outpost. Infrequently, they passed high dunes of sand that slapped against the wall in spots where she could safely descend to the desert floor, but it was far easier on her legs to keep to the solid walkway atop the hub wall. The light of dawn swept across the desert horizon, broken only by the silhouette of the central station left far behind. Miles later, they came across an antenna array which provided a meager amount of shade from the blazing twin suns rising overhead.

Ala took that as her cue to grab another meal out of BoB's compartment and take a rest, while assuring herself, that with a little luck, she could take a refreshing ionic shower by the end of the day aboard her own ship. It was eating away at her conscience whether she should still risk trying to fill her holding tanks with water and make off like a bandit, but if any of these rogue bots popped a hole in her ship, she would be entirely screwed. As she ground the soft protein meal packet between her teeth, Ala figured the latter was the wisest choice. She could always sell the information about this deserted complex and collect her finder's fee for providing valuable coordinates and data on the abandoned site to another group of scavengers.

"Bob, I was wondering if your weaponry can be deactivated?" She asked, sitting in the thin shade of the antenna base while sipping on a bag of filtered water.

"I can at will, but such an action wouldn't be advisable in our current scenario," the droid advised.

"No, what I mean is, can it be physically deactivated to keep it from being re-engaged?" Ala asked, waffling on the idea of storing BoB in the ships hold on her trip back. The robotic model they put him in was far too large to wander the rest of the ship anyhow.

"Actually, Ala, I have kept reminding you that I need to go offline for several hours to do a full diagnosis of my systems. I still do not know the complete functions of this new robotic shell they stuffed me into," he reminded her in a huff. "I would recommend that you should also initiate a self-diagnostic, as it seems your own memory might require a bit of corrective defragmenting," BoB offered politely, but Ala didn't take it that way.

"Look here you bag of bolts..." she started to argue.

"*Bucket* of Bolts," The droid quickly interrupted to correct, only to be met by her disgruntled glare.

"Human minds don't work that way. Sometimes we forget shit, and sometimes we remember crap we would much rather forget!" She trailed off in a gentler tone when the thought of her mother came to mind.

BoB sat silently for a moment calculating in deep thought; figuring it must be a terrible thing to be human, especially since they could not dump chunks of memory at will whenever it was no longer wanted nor used, and were only left to be haunted by these ghosts of data for the rest of their operational life. With her internal systems so grievously fragmented, it was no wonder Ala acted the way she did ...a pity indeed.

Hidden behind the glare of the rising suns, a lone figure limped down the path towards the two companions. The heat trail of Ala's bare footprints began to wash away in the morning light, but the Reaper knew he was on the right track. His embedded motion sensors had a very limited range, but his high-function AI was programmed to keep track of its prey. He could see his target in the distance. A single human controller that seemed to be in the custody of another large three-legged droid of a design he failed to recognize.

Messenger

Her bare breasts glistened with sweat as Ala laid down for a moment to rest. BoB stood beside her, trying to familiarize himself with his internal programs while he had the spare time. His new systems were extremely complicated; not at all like the simple grid patterns his original data platform had been used to processing. His former existence had been designed for taking minor test samples of soil and reporting them back to the station hubs for analysis. Digital charts had supplemented his ability to measure distance with pinpoint accuracy over difficult and hostile terrain. However, this new body was a mystery, and it was actually very annoying to have to decipher visual data from an array of multiple optical eyes and wasted far too much effort simply to calculate his center of gravity with every step.

After his AI core was installed into this spider tank shell, BoB had overridden his newly-installed program banks, then immediately reattached his protected memory chips and ran off to rescue Ala from her incarceration at the neglected pumping station. BoB disapproved of this heavy mass he had been installed into, for it lacked the freedom he had become so accustomed to. This body was designed as a weapon and served no other purpose but for warring against enemy factions. The mounted cannons on his dome did worry him a little, since he had no idea what their range was, or how to fire them with any measure of safety or accuracy.

Ala closed her eyes and drifted off for a few moments, absorbing the aroma of the warm sand that drifted in the hot breeze. She shaded her eyes with one hand as she turned over to look at the rising twin suns to estimate how long it would be before the blazing heat of noon. A spec in the distance caught her eye; though at first, she thought it was a mirage; the silhouette of a dark figure wavering in the rising heat. She laid there for a long time wondering if what she was seeing was real or if the harsh light was playing tricks on her. Squinting against the bright sunlight glaring behind it, she finally turned to ask her companion what he could make of the strange object.

BoB spun his dome around and peered into the distance, straight across the path they had already covered along the high wall. He did not recognize the object at all, it appeared to be something human; but not. It walked upright on two thin legs with double-jointed knees that were mere skeletal framework; its feet were wide and distinctly clawed, designed to function in multiple types of terrain. It walked in an odd way, as if it was favoring one of its legs. With a quick reference to his data spool, it appeared there was no current visual diagram on record of the robotic unit that was approaching their position.

Ala sat up while squinting her eyes to block out the harsh sunlight, and when the figure moved its left arm upward she saw the flash of a long blade. She immediately felt her stomach sink. Images of all those dead bodies she had seen back in the colony ship flooded back into her head and the vision of its horrid metal mask that had lain buried there in the mound of decaying flesh. But that bot was dead, deactivated; wasn't it? Had there been others like it at the base station? As a drop of sweat rolled down her cheek, it began to make sense. It dawned on her that this soldier droid was what those voices had been calling to …this messenger of death.

Ala jumped for her gun.

"Bob, shoot it; blast it with your cannon!" The girl screamed. The spider droid spun his dome around to look at her in confusion.

"It might be non-hostile. It seems to be alone; we should try to communicate with…" he never finished as Ala interrupted.

"It's a G series, asshole! One of those Reaper things that wiped out the colonists!" She spat back at him as fear slowly mounted in her with every step it took. BoB took a short moment to access the sub-file on the hunter units before he blurted out a response.

"Oh sh-it," he uttered, having learned the colorful word from the girls common speech, "…but that model was decommissioned decades ago," BoB seemed confused.

"I saw one in that crashed transport shuttle where I picked this up," Ala motioned with a wave of her silver pulse gun, "there might be several more that have been hiding who-knows-where? Stop asking questions and just blast the fucking thing, would you!" Ala yelled at him. BoB responded by clicking his forward gun to the ready, the dreaded Arch Cannon in his arsenal. His legs tilted forward as he braced to absorb the shock; as this was the first run of his firing systems, though he wasn't familiar with their proper sequence as yet.

Ala wished she would have taken cover, as her proximity to the blast and resulting blowback from the muzzle nearly deafened her. BoB remembered what actions the other spider tank models had taken during the battle the previous night, and he had to make a rough guess at the firing sequence since his human companion had busted his motion sensors days before, and as a result, it now appeared that his automated targeting array was malfunctioning. His shot went too long. The arch of plasma rose high into the morning sky, then exploded at its peak; it was much less impressive to watch in the daylight. The deadly shower of primed particles fell harmlessly back into the dunes far past his target; his aim was off and had gone astray. The Hellbot hadn't even noticed as the ion shrapnel landed far behind him.

"Oops," BoB responded, as he loaded another round; trying to correct his trajectory for a second try. This time, Ala jumped back and covered her ears, as her head was still ringing from his first shot.

Another blast fired from his forward muzzle, arching high into the sky. On this attempt, the charged particles showered down in the correct line of sight, but he had still overshot by several yards.

"I don't believe this is the most accurate of weapons," He explained.

"Don't you have a targeting system somewhere in that tin can?" Ala slammed the butt of her gun against his dome with transparent aggravation, "Aim lower!" She screamed.

BoB appeared nervous as he shifted his dome and tried to steady his legs again for another volley, not wishing to suffer her wrath should he miss again; which he did. The spider bot was learning these awkward manual systems on the fly. The blast fired and exploded on impact a few dozen feet in front of the approaching android. The explosion ripped a hole in the floor of the wall, revealing a dark cavity beneath. Staring at the damage, they came to realize that this hub wall they had been walking on, was actually a covered tunnel.

The Hellbot stopped short, as it was now perfectly clear that the three-legged droid that held the human captive had hostile intentions towards him, and was not going to cooperate with the termination of its prisoner. The android caught his balance as the blast in front of him rocked the walkway. His thermal eye caught a glimpse of the rail system below. Much of the debris had fallen into the small chasm, but there was still adequate room to circumvent the gaping hole to reach his target.

If his leg joints had not been so badly damaged, he could have easily jumped the gap in a single stride. The Reaper observed BoB readying a stance to fire another round; but stalled. Logically, the robot's targeting systems must have been malfunctioning, either that or it had been intentionally firing warning shots in his direction, which didn't make any logical sense. With a spurt of energy, the Reaper picked up speed to close the distance between them when he observed the spider bot rotating its smaller caliber gun towards him.

"Use the other one!" Ala had yelled back at BoB, who took a quick glance in her direction, then spun his rear AG gun at their approaching foe. It was a lower caliber firearm, but was far more accurate. Turning his attention back to the Hellbot, he saw it rushing at them in staggered leaps and bounds. The Reaper was specially designed with a rail-thin midsection and rounded hip joints to help deflect weapons fire, making it an extremely difficult target to hit.

Frantically, BoB let off a volley of wild shots. One round struck the advancing droid in the air during mid-stride, flipping it end over end. The spinning android hit the ground several meters behind where it had been clipped, and its metal body slid along the walkway until it dropped into the gaping hole of the damaged corridor.

There was the sound of a crash below, followed by an

eerie silence. Ala couldn't believe it was that easy and dared to take a few steps towards the edge to verify that the bot was dead.

"Ala, wait, I'm still reading an electronic signature..." BoB warned from behind, just as the Hellbot leaped back up to the surface on its double-jointed legs. It stood there brooding, wobbling on its damaged left leg as sparks flew from its hip joint. It knew its movement had been severely impaired by that lucky shot, but that was of no consequence; for it was within firing range now.

It's first target was to ensure the deactivation of the human, and then it would turn its attention to this insolent droid that had been taking pop shots at it. He raised his forearm and fired at the girl. BoB knocked Ala over as he dodged in the way of the blast, his spider model body having the advantage of an exceptional level of dexterity. The round bounced harmlessly off his domed shell. Ala screamed as she rolled out of the way of BoB's deadly sharp legs clacking the ground around her like metal spears as he steadied his footing. The Reaper took another shot, only to be met by another block; this one costing BoB one of his optical eyes, which exploded in a puff of pulverized glass and smoke.

Pulse rounds were highly inefficient on other droids, and the Hellbot knew his options were few. It became clear he would have to first remove this large bot that had become such a nuisance. Ripping it apart would be an easy task for its long scythe blade. The Reaper found a certain satisfaction in his programmed duties; especially when it came to using his lance. It was a generally useless appendage save for one purpose; causing violent structural damage. It was made of heavy alloys that could cleave through most other metals, and articulate enough to make sweeping strikes at any angle.

BoB rotated his dome to point the AG gun at the Reaper, who countered his move by dodging in the opposite direction. The mounted guns of the spider droid were not designed to be used at such close range and the Hellbot had moved within the blind spot beside him. BoB let a few rounds rip free, which zipped harmlessly over the head of the Reaper as it weaved and dodged. It was trying to make its way past the defensive area of the droid's long legs so he could make a mortal blow at the core circuitry within his domed shell.

BoB had to back up quickly as Ala jumped to the side behind him. The Hellbot took a swing, only to catch its blade arm deep within the spider's foremost limb. It struggled there for a fraction of a second, realizing its mistake. Ala almost hesitated, but managed to spin her own pulse gun around to take aim as the Hellbot glared at her with its single red eye. She let loose several shots; however, the Reaper's armored cowl was created for such defense, and it twisted to protect its vital head sensors. The thing was designed like a medieval knight, with the only vulnerable area being its visual array. The shots from her pulse gun ricocheted harmlessly off its thick armor plating.

After her volley, it raised its own firearm and took aim at her head in return. BoB could not shield her in time, as his leg was weighted down by the killer droid whose scythe was stuck in his appendage. His only tactical option was to sharply alter the dynamics of their current proximity; calculated in mere milliseconds by his computerized brain, BoB lifted his sliced foreleg up with a flick, dragging the attached android along with it. The Reaper jerked, and his shot at the girl had fired wild as he was thrown high into the air. The tension on his arm-blade finally released, and he was flung over the high wall into the dunes below.

Inspecting the cosmetic damage of his forelimb, BoB tested its ability to hold his weight. He knew full well that the one design flaw of his model would leave him immobile if even a single leg should become damaged. Ala didn't dare to look over the outer ledge, but took a curious peek at the hole in the walkway. This entire hub wall encased a rail system used for cargo transports; it must lead to the lower level of Outpost 9 where the water storage tanks had been. They could now see that this corridor housed the plumbing needed to service the central facility.

BoB advised that he could not fire over the wall at this angle, and that it was their best option to make a run for it. It didn't take more than a few seconds for Ala to realize there was no way she could maintain a running pace in this heat for long, nor could she see the tower of the outlying station anywhere in the near distance. They had to destroy that Hellbot, but how many more were coming for her? Ala took a quick inspection of BoB's broken eyepiece.

"It's not so bad; besides, you've got a dozen others," she muttered in her failed attempt to console him, "that thing is too well armored for my little pea shooter, you're gonna have to take this one on your own," she instructed the droid. However, BoB was not entirely confident he could do so. From the lower wall they heard the sounds of violent slashing, and the androids aggravated speech translated through her implant.

"*I will destroy it!*" the Reaper cursed in a maniacal voice as it ripped a foothold into the side of the wall with its sharp blade. For lack of hands, it had chopped out horizontal steps for its clawed feet to take hold as it climbed up the slanted wall to reach them. Seeing this, BoB took a few cautious steps back.

"Actually, Ala, I fear you might get caught in the crossfire. These cannon units I'm equipped with are not designed for close-range use," the droid confessed.

The twin suns beat down upon the surface of the walkway; waves of rising heat distorting the desert plain. She could still see the tall spires of the main complex beyond, now the stronghold of these enraged bots. The vast sea of dunes that surrounded them was an ironic testament to the infertile efforts of mankind to synthesize their own Eden. The Avalon project; named after a legendary island of paradise from ancient lore, was encompassed here by an ocean of drifting sand. The colonist's efforts to expand their habitat and alter this entire ecosystem had led them to their graves; victims of their own technology. Instead of a garden, they had turned Tranquility into a tomb.

The gleam of a blade pierced into the upper edge of the walkway as the combat droid breached the top. Ala jumped for cover as BoB rotated his AG cannon towards the threat, letting off a spray of weapons fire. The energy beams showered over the area as the Hellbot ducked for cover, then rolled and launched itself onto the deck in one fluid motion. Before the arachnid droid could realign its cannon, the Hellbot took a vicious swipe; cleaving the bottom tip of BoB's forward leg in two. The wound to his structure severely altered his balance, and his volley shot low; peppering the floor at the clawed feet of the murderous Reaper.

BoB struggled to right himself, discovering his loss of

balance proved to be more detrimental to his systems than he would have expected. Ala tried to buy him some time by plugging in a few shots of her own, which only served as a mild annoyance to the hooded droid; though it did pause to turn its attention towards her once again.

"*Your head is mine*," it glared, speaking in a strange blocky tone. Ala's binary implant picked up the threat as clear as a bell. BoB had also heard these menacing words; and his combat program selected this verbal clue, one that matched his weapons systems.

<DEPLOY MINES> Highlighted in his internal array. Without hesitation, BoB stood entirely erect; just as the Reaper lunged forward to carve its long blade into the arachnids dome, his three long legs straightened out, leaving his main body to teeter high above the other bot. He was unable to maintain the balance for more than a few seconds, as one limb had been chopped shorter than the others; but the Hellbot did take a moment to try to decipher this strange behavior.

Like a stone, the weight of BoB's dome came crashing down on the combat droid, catching its blade arm under its weight; pinning him. Like fine clockwork, tiny gears whirred as dual-port doors flipped down small ramps. From the dark compartments within swarmed dozens of miniature droid spiders that magnetically attached themselves to the trapped android. After they deployed, the automated compartments closed and let BoB rise upon his feet. Ala and her companion backed away as the horde of tiny droids clipped to every exposed inch of the Reaper who struggled to stand; covered from his hooded head to clawed foot in miniature spider mines.

"Dispose of your firearm, Ala, those mines are reverse polarized to my shell alone," BoB warned the girl as she quickly flung her weapon over the side of the wall.

The Hellbot attempted to raise its gun to take a shot at the girl, but its forearm was caught in the interlocked extremities of the multiple mini-droids encasing it. Its blade arm was weighed down, unable to move. The android stumbled on its broken hip and fell. The initial explosion cracked the weakened walkway and a wide crevice ripped open where it had been struck by weapons fire. Within a fraction of a second, the other armed mines began to detonate in tandem as the ensnared Reaper rolled across the surface.

The edge of the foundation collapsed, dropping the Hellbot into the railway chamber below. With a thundering explosion, the tunnel erupted into a cloud of fire. The entire walkway shook, knocking Ala and BoB off their feet. Moments later, fine bits of dust and debris rained back down upon the upper deck as the two companions sought protection. Covering her mouth, the wind shifted and Ala tried to keep from breathing the acrid smoke that enveloped them.

"Holy shit!" She coughed as she dared to tiptoe near the edge of the smoking hole; testing its structural integrity. "What a way to shoot your wad," Ala smirked; although the sexual pun was entirely lost upon the confused droid.

"I'm not sure what that means…" BoB responded, still a bit dazed by the explosion. Ala just laughed. Once the thick smoke dispersed, they could see through the blackened soot of the shattered railway below. They couldn't make out any pieces that looked like the android except for a long single blade embedded in the opposite wall. Though the corridor beneath them was a disastrous mess, with a little effort, Ala climbed down into the chamber tunnel. They could follow this route to the station without having to bake under the heat of the twin suns. BoB agreed this route was best, since they would be out of sight from the surface in case any more droids should come looking for them.

Thick pipes lined the corridor; many were bent and deformed from the explosion. Torn fiber optics bundles and broken tubing littered the floor around the monorail. Underneath the grating she could see a large pipe leading down its length, likely used by the aquifer pumps from the water station. The tunnel was dark, but at least it would provide shelter from the searing heat outside. Plus, there would be no chance of losing their way or being spotted by other droid patrols.

There wasn't much room for BoB to maneuver, and the air seemed a bit stale as the foul taint of decay still lingered within. BoB advised her that it was likely that the explosion would attract the attention of any droid units in the area, so they should make haste to their destination. Within the tunnel, broken pipes and cables hung from the ceiling and walls from several decades of neglected maintenance. Buildings like these were made from plasti-cement, which was a form of waterless concrete commonly used in colony habitats. With the proper resources, alloy metals were fabricated on site to provide internal bracing and protective surface plating.

The dim musty tunnel echoed with strange sounds and creaks from the force of the wind blowing topside. It wasn't very cheery down in this gloom, but it was a nice break from the heat of the desert. However, if any more bots were bright enough to follow them down into this corridor there would be no means of escape.

There had been power at the station the last time she was there; the real question was if her ship was still waiting topside. The AI computer on the Valkyrie was decent for computing navigational arrays and chart logging for light jumps, and possessed a bit of a snooty personality as far as Ala was concerned, however, its range of protocols for practicing common sense was pretty much limited to flight calculations. Ala was starting to feel nervous about finally getting to the outpost to see if she still had a ride home, which was a term she used loosely since she had no real place to call home in the cosmos except for the belly of her ship.

It was too bad the soil transformation project hadn't worked, Ala thought to herself as they trudged down the dark corridor, this place could have been made into a real sanctuary by now. If it hadn't been for the mysterious sequence of events these colonists had suffered, this planet might have made a positive mark in the universe. Near one-to-one earth gravity planets were difficult enough to find as it was, but stumbling across one with a breathable atmosphere and vegetation that could be nurtured by atmospheric rains would be a dream come true for every spacer left lost among the darkness between the stars.

For a brief moment, she understood what it was these colonists had been dreaming of, a real place to call home without being encased in claustrophobic artificial environments and crowded habitats like countless others dotted across the universe. They wanted to regain something that had only been familiar to their ancestors, the lost images of a green Earth ...but there was no chance of that here, not now.

Several miles in, BoB spotted something with his infrared filter. There was an object lying in the middle of the tunnel by the rails. By the dim red glow of BoB's optics, Ala made her way towards the huddled object. It turned out to be the body of another colonist; at least this one still had its head. It was lying directly under another antenna junction where a chute with a ladder rose up the far wall. Ala tried to get topside, but the hatch was stuck; likely rusted solid or covered with sand. The dead colonist appeared to be wearing a pale white technician's uniform; much like the one Renee had worn. Beside him there sat a digital tablet.

The device was dead, but BoB was able to provide a hotwire from his own energy core, and since his own circuitry was from the same era, their technology was still compatible. Recharging the battery chip took only minutes. It turned out to be the log results from the drilling cage that transported from each platform site. Its specs showed it to be a monster of a machine that used pulse energy lasers to bore into the subsurface. The personal log he left on the device explained why they had found his body lying here in limbo between the two complex sites along the rim of the outer hub.

"Drilling at station 21 started yesterday. There seems to be an abundance of shallow underground caves in this region and we made sure it was placed directly above the natural cavity as we did at several of the other sites. The tanks from outpost 8 and 9 were sent in by auto-rail for cleansing before the last three bore sites are completed next month. The head executives from REVO will be arriving next week to review the progress on the soil transformation, which has hit a few snags recently but it's nothing we can't correct. The real problem is the soil filtration, because if that doesn't work, then that's several years of wasted labor up in smoke, so to say."

The log ended, flipping to the next entry, "There's been

a glitch in the rail system to several of the outposts, likely a problem due to static electricity from the atmospheric processors. The project is currently entering a critical stage as we are trying to seed the new clouds to produce rain so it can be tested for acidity levels. We need to get that issue ironed out before the suits get here, or the base commander will have our necks if we embarrass him," the log switched again, though the man never bothered to give his name on the recordings.

"I've been sent to do a visual inspection of each of the access tunnels. Rail tubes 1 through 4, 6, and 8 are running, but the rest seem to be offline, as the carts are losing power. Our droid tech sent out a few drones to scan the corridors for any damage yesterday, but anyone can tell you that those robotic units aren't exactly known to be the brightest crayons in the box, so the Boss sent me out for a hands-on inspection," he finished on a high note as the log switched once again, "The personnel stationed at Outpost 5, 7 and 9 have reported seeing odd lights and other phenomena, which I would guess are electrical surges from the ground static. I'm leaving station 7 now for tube 9."

The record ended with an automated alert of an approaching storm front, warning that all personnel were to evacuate the rail tubes. Apparently, this poor guy had been caught in the middle of nowhere and may have tried to get topside. Static electricity in the megawatts could have flashed down this funnel and fried him; but now his body was so decimated by time that there was no way to tell what had actually killed him. If he was lucky, it had been over for him quickly. Hopefully, someone had left the door unlocked for him on the other side of the tunnel. Ala snatched the access key that was hanging around his neck, just in case.

She respectfully scooted his body to the side with a gentle push of her feet and left his desiccated remains behind. It wasn't far until BoB noted that the tunnel had began to slope, the incline was so slight that Ala hadn't even noticed. As BoB was limping along on his broken foreleg, Ala made a mental note to see if they could find something to repair him.

"I have some hot-fix tools on my ship, they're usually used to cut apart orbiting wrecks and other types of salvaged equipment, but I can weld you together with them just the same," Ala assured him with a pat on his damaged leg. It would be something simple to repair, for she was handy with the tools of her trade. The farther they descended below ground the air became noticeably cooler. Long before they reached the end of the rail, BoB detected the loading bay situated in the darkness beyond. There they found a number of empty crates and barrels, including several lengths of replacement tubing. A large wheeled cart sitting to one side, which appeared to be what they used to move the tanks; behind it was a slotted panel beside a set of thick double doors, upon which Ala used the access key she had recently acquired.

Truthfully though, she was a bit nervous about entering the lower section of the outpost once again, fearing that whatever force had knocked her out and transported her into the middle of the desert might still be inside. Ala felt suddenly weak in her knees and sat for a moment to explain to BoB what had happened to her for the first time. He wasn't programmed to theorize on paranormal activity; such anomalies were simply unknown events and he could not logically apply fear or superstition to their evaluations.

The sad truth was; Ala was afraid of things beyond her control. The death of her parents and the countless dead and forgotten from the salvage jobs she had pulled over the years …it had all left a deep scar upon her conscience. Ala's recent experiences on Tranquility were the icing on the cake. Over recent years, Ala couldn't help but notice that no matter where she went in the galaxy, she never got the feeling of being somewhere she belonged. All the shanty towns and run down habitats on backwater planets, or even under the glossy lighting in deep space colony stations; all the people looked awkwardly sad and displaced …as though they were lost souls searching for a purpose. It was an underlying tone that seemed to weigh their every step. No one wanted to put it into plain words; they were mourning the loss of Earth, as if we torched our own sacred home and were left with no other choice but to cast our bodies out into the dark winter of space.

There were so many systems, so many worlds; but none of them were where we truly belonged. Like the rest of the human race, Ala, herself, could not see through the veil of it. It was as if the human psyche was wired to lie to itself, even in the face of the inevitable. It was the actions of billions of people centuries ago and the events that followed that led her to be at this door, suffering what she had all these years like thousands of other spacers peppered throughout the galaxy. Once she got back to her ship, where was she going to go?

Ala just wanted to get off this damn rock; a sonic shower and a decent meal would do her good. Jet off into orbit and sleep in her own cramped bed to catch up on some rest and she would worry about it all tomorrow. That was the only way she knew how to live, as one day blurred into the next. Breaking the silence, BoB hit her with a harsh question that snapped the girl out of her wallow of self-pity.

"Will you take me with you, Ala ...when you leave?" It was a cold, almost sad tone from the droid; a question she didn't want to answer. The young pilot stuttered, searching for some excuse not to give a definitive reply. She was used to being alone, and that was the meat of it. Even if she could somehow manually disable BoB's internal firing systems and secure him within the hold of her ship, she would only end up either selling him to some back-planet junkyard or a second-rate collector for a few spare credits.

Here she was, wondering what a metal bot was going to think of her. Had she gone soft ...or was she just a cold bitch to begin with?

"I'll see what I can do," she flew off with an excuse, "but let's see if my ship is still there first, shall we?" She cut her answer short, angry at herself for lying to her mechanical friend. The question was; did she owe this box of metal anything? BoB wasn't a real person after all, he was just a machine ...there's was a difference; right? Ala wasn't great at handling emotions; she had learned to avoid them since she was a child and relied on her practiced talent of being insensitive for lack of knowing how to face her bottled feelings. BoB had survived here since before she was born; would it really be fair to rescue him from this rock only to abandon him on some inbred colony planet and sell him off as a mere slave-droid or spare parts? She didn't want to think about it.

She quickly changed the subject and had BoB help her get the doors open when the power clicked on in the panel, as the sliding hinge was jammed full of grit and sand. After breaching the entry, they found that the curved hallway beyond led to a lower level. Ala didn't recognize this area. She wanted to go up, not down; and was paranoid about entering that underground cavern again for good reason. There was plenty of water in that subterranean pool to siphon, but she didn't want to risk having to wind up going through this whole ordeal all over again. She wasn't even exactly sure *what* exactly had happen, but the thought of it spooked her.

With a foreboding afterthought, she broke off her stare from the long dark hall that led to the lower level. She turned left and made her way off the ramp towards the ground floor. With timid apprehension, she stepped into the control room to find the female corpse was still lying there undisturbed where she had left it. The console she had previously used was dark, as it had automatically powered down. BoB clanked along behind her in the tight corridor as she made her way back to the exterior hatch. With a hard jimmy at the rusted door; it seemed to have gotten stuck again since she had last entered. High piles of sand flowed in when it finally pried opened with a creak and warm sunlight poured over her face as she stepped out into the dusty plain.

This hatch was far too small for BoB to fit through so she instructed him to wait for her. The girl remembered seeing an access door at the back of the station during landing and assured him there was a rear cargo bay that would allow him to get outside. First item of order was to prep her ship. Walking out into the field of dunes, she took a long stroll into the hot desert; shielding her eyes from the bright twin suns overhead. The weary girl spun once and ran over another dune, and another, as a stab of panic began to set in ...her goddamn ship was gone!

"What the fuck ...no, no, no!" She cried softly.

Ala sank to her knees in the hot sand, feeling suddenly ill and lightheaded. She had made it all this way just to find that she was stranded here. She sat there for a long quiet moment as wisps of dust washed over the dunes, looking out over the rolling landscape with despair. With a glint of light catching her attention, she shaded her eyes from the harsh rays of the twin suns. A thick cloud of dust, carried upon the desert breeze, slowly subsided, and exposed the aft side of the Valkyrie set behind the observation deck of the outpost. Not believing her eyes, Ala stood and gave a yelp of glee, although gravely worried if the ship was still in one piece.

She ran down the dune and made her way around the foundation of the station, frantically climbing over the beds of loose sand. Her ship was parked a ways behind the back entry of the outpost, partially buried in the dunes. That bothered her a bit, as this was certainly not where she had left it. The ship seemed to be undamaged, though slightly tarnished by patches of oxidation on the hull. Her remote had been lost since this whole ordeal began, so Ala had to hike her way over to the sealed bay door. The ship's AI would have secured the ramp after a given timeframe, so that wasn't terribly unusual; but she noted several large patches of alien rust now lining the exterior of the ship.

She found the beveled cube of the hatch panel, which slowly activated after a curious pause. She punched in her code and spoke to the computer.

"Val, it's me, open up," Ala said with a sigh of relief. After an odd delay, she heard a few of the ships systems power up from within the hull. Finally, the computers voice came back online, accompanied by a fair deal of crackled static.

"*Zzzzt, krrt* ...voice recognition authorized, welcome aboard, Ala," Valaria conveyed in her usual pleasant tone as the gears of the bay door struggled to cycle open, while lowering the ramp to let her to climb in. She shut the hatch door after boarding and made her way to the deck level. Everything was where she had left it, all except the position of the ship.

"Why did you move from my parking spot," Ala inquired while wiping the sweat from her brow, "...you really had me worried there for a moment."

"There have been several sandstorms in this sector since the time you departed, Ala; and without further orders, I determined it was safer to move the Valkyrie behind the adjacent structure to protect it from the high winds."

"Ah, you were letting the building take the brunt of it?"

"That is correct Ala," the computer confirmed.

"Did anything strange happen while I was gone?" The girl asked casually as she grabbed her shirt and clothes lying on the floor to put them on, though noting they seemed unusually musty, "The air smells pretty stale in here, did you take the scrubbers offline?" She wondered aloud while sniffing the front of her shirt. Then again, maybe she was just smelling her own lingering stench in the cabin, which Ala figured she might notice after spending the past few weeks outside in the open air.

"Please define *strange*," Valaria retorted in her usual curt tone, "there were a number of recorded incidents that may, or may not, fit that category," the computer conceded as Ala noticed the fine film of dust lining the cockpit panels. She knew that damn sand would find its way in through the ducts, and it would cost her quite a few credits to have that oxidation scrubbed from the hull once she got back to a spaceport. With a sigh, she wondered where she was going to get the funds for that. She would have to pull off another few jobs, but those were few and far between lately, since the number of spacers this side of the galaxy had dramatically dwindled, "And yes, Ala, I deactivated the ventilation and O_2 scrubbers, and placed them offline due to your extended absence," Valaria confessed.

"What for? I've only been gone a week or two at best," she blurted in confusion while slowly noticing the rancid smell that was emanating from the food locker. Ala suddenly froze, her eyes wide with confusion as she was stunned by the computer's response.

"That is incorrect. Actually, Ala, by the standard Terran calendar it has been over 856 days since you departed."

Entity

Ala was confounded, rattled to the point of refusing to believe what Valaria had just told her. Despite the irrational claim, she remembered the computer doesn't lie, it just spits out facts; that still didn't keep the bewildered girl from tripping over her words.

"Wa... what?" She mumbled in astonishment.

"You have been gone two Terran solar years, four months and four days, would you also like the hour count, Ala?" Valaria answered in what came across to Ala as a smug tone.

"No! There's no fucking way ...how is that possible?" She spat.

"Could you please rephrase the question, Ala, I don't believe you are entirely uneducated with the function of date calculations," the computer responded immediately. The smell of her clothes, the rotting food locker, the caked dust, how had that much time passed without her noticing? Then she remembered her abduction, the strange dream and being left abandoned in the desert. What the hell was going on here? Ala simply had enough; she couldn't take any more of this shit.

"How are the power core levels?" she demanded.

"Optimal, but there has been a slight systems drain, though it is still well above 60%," Valaria advised. Ala remembered she had burned up a great deal of energy from the plasma core on the jump out here, and into the system belt. Still, it was enough to get her back to Pandora. She took a short moment as her thoughts lingered on BoB, who was still waiting for her at the cargo bay inside the station but there was no way she was going to stay on this accursed sandbox for another second; BoB could take care of himself.

"I want you to prep for immediate launch and calculate a trajectory back to Pandora, and get the Freezer ready for me, Val," Ala ordered, putting her hand over her eyes to suppress the headache that had manifested itself in the past few minutes.

"I can't do that, Ala," the AI responded flatly. The young pilot just sat there rubbing the bridge of her nose with her eyes clenched, trying to absorb the absurdity of her situation. Ala thought she had misheard her.

"What?" She whispered, trying to soothe the throbbing in her head as she rubbed her temples.

"I said, I can't do that," Valaria repeated.

"Prep the Freezer and let's liftoff this fucking rock the moment the engines are primed, and don't wake me until we're back in the Aries system!" The girl's voice rose in anger; having lost any form of patience to put up with Valaria's attitude. She just wanted to drown herself in cryo-stasis and forget this whole fucking nightmare had ever happened.

"Negative, Ala," the ship responded.

Slapping her hands down onto the control board in frustration, Ala began to punch in the launch sequence herself. A moment later, the entire board went black as the power cut from the control panel with a dying hum. The young pilot was aghast.

"Launch aborted," Valaria advised the stunned girl who sat in the captain's chair, "...my new prime directives prevent me from aiding you, Ala," the computer advised.

The drumming in her head got worse and worse until she jumped up to the medical cabinet to take a hypo, only to find two empty cylinders from the ones she had used just before landing. Somehow, within the past two years, her ships' onboard AI had been tainted by the alien anomaly and somehow reprogrammed. She considered for a wild moment of yanking out the computer's circuitry and flying out of here manually, but the AI systems were wired into every part of the ship, let alone, it would have been impossible for her to cipher a light jump back to the space lanes. She was enslaved by the level of technology of her time, there was no way around it; she was stuck here.

Ala opened her mouth to start a heated debate with the computer about what was, and was not, its prime directives and who was the captain of this ship; but in the breadth of a nanosecond, Ala had lost her steam. There would be no winning a dispute with the malfunctioning computer. At least it had let her onboard to grab some fucking clothes. Ala tore apart the maintenance panel and hotwired the sonic shower so she wouldn't have to ask Valaria to turn it on, lest it deny her that one luxury. Her favorite set of clothes and her blaster were still gone, lost somewhere back in that water-filled cave beneath the station. After tenderly wrapping her dry callused feet, she threw on a spare outfit and an extra pair of boots.

The young Scavy lay there on her bed, tossing and turning in distress as she tried to figure out what to do. There was no way to rewire the ship to disable the AI; and even if she could, she would likely kill herself and destroy the ship attempting a manual jump with the light drive. Two years of her life had been stolen. Looking into the mirror, she tried to see if she had aged, but there were only the fine wrinkles from exposure to the dry desert heat. The time must have passed when she had been abducted. Insomnia set in and she floundered there in the thermal sheets until she nearly lost her mind. She had become a prisoner on this forsaken moon.

Ala realized that she couldn't hide in the ship forever, and it was only a matter of time before more of those Reapers or any number of droid patrols would finally hunt her down. She needed answers, and there was only one place she knew where to find them; this had all started when she had stumbled upon that cave below the outpost station. She didn't have a spare blaster that worked, only a long boot knife. All her rations onboard had long since expired. She realized that she had to go back inside; whatever had happened to her within that subterranean grotto was at the center of this mystery.

She lowered the ramp and stormed off the ship, back out into the heart of the shifting sands. The sunlight waned as Thebes began to drift across the sky, its soft shadows spreading across the surface of Tranquility; nightfall would soon be approaching. Climbing her way over the steep slopes around the perimeter, she finally made it back to the forward hatch of the station; only to find that BoB wasn't there.

At least she had mind enough to take a pair of lights with her this time, which she had strapped to the back of her hands. Storming down the hall with what bravery she could muster, Ala made her way back into the control room to check the station diagram once again. Tracing her way to the rear bay cargo doors, she found several empty storage containers but her droid companion was nowhere to be found. Down on the lower levels, she finally inspected the storage room that once held the silo tanks, but still no BoB. For a moment, she wondered if he had deserted her and headed back out through the rail tunnel. She had actually left him waiting for several hours and felt a twinge of guilt for considering to leave him here to rot; it was certainly a selfish motive that backfired on her.

Making her way back up to the hallway panel that led into the subterranean cavern, she timidly triggered the door sensor to open. She tapped on her palm lights and made her way down the corridor of bluish alien rock that was rippled with layered veins. Within the cavern, she found the large droid sitting on the bank beside the pool of still water. Ala approached the bot and began to apologize for leaving him waiting for so long, but BoB didn't even acknowledge her presence. It took her a moment to notice that his eyes were dark and that he had completely powered down.

The dripping water echoed through the small cavern, its calm waters were eerily clear. The glow from her hand lights reflected off the moist rock, glittering across the room. She stood there in silence, and for just a brief moment, Ala felt at peace. As out of place as the feeling was, it tugged at her in a way that made her heart ache with a sense of loss.

"I'm here," she finally called out into the silence of the cave, "…what do you want from me?" Ala pleaded.

There was a strange stillness to the air, but then a dim glow from deep below the surface of the pool began to rise. Ala stepped back, fighting the urge to run in fear; though realizing she had nowhere to go. The soft glowing light broke through the surface, an orb of cold fire like a miniature blue sun floating there above the tranquil pool. The sphere wasn't blinding this time or aflame with violent arcs of electricity but slowly transformed into the likeness of a woman. When this apparition had appeared before, Ala had thought it was the ghost of the dead technician in the control room, but she had been mistaken; the image resembled Ala, herself!

Its arms beckoned once and lowered, motioning towards the pool below. The young girl didn't know what she was seeing, but this strange entity had not abducted her in a flash of light as before. Ala pulled off her boots and constrictive clothing and stepped into the edge of the pool. Taking a deep breath, she dove into the blue depths, the glow of her palm lights lighting the darkness. She didn't know what she was searching for; all she remembered was the impossibly vast cavern she had seen in a vision. Ala was lost; if she was to drown here on this desolate desert planet, it would be an ironic end to her sorry existence.

The sapphire waters engulfed her, this cavern basin proving to be deeper than she could have ever imagined. Mild currents tugged and flowed as bubbles rose towards the surface lost above, surrounding her in a spiraling cascade. There was nothing down here but a maze of underwater streams pulsing through this living world. She felt weak, knowing she had to break for the surface, but couldn't find the energy that had been sapped from her limbs. All this precious water she had traveled so very far to claim, was now killing her. The last of her breath escaped her lips and a shuddering calm overtook her. Death wasn't as she had expected it would be; she felt detached from the swelling pain in her lungs as her body went numb.

A consuming force drew her limp body down into the fathomless depths. It was as if the pool itself had taken the girl, capturing her in its cold embrace. The waters filled Ala's lungs, invading her body; claiming her as its own. Ala knew she had died …but somehow, she awoke from the darkness that tugged at her very soul.

Ala found herself on the same precipice as before in that distant dream. Heaving to purge the water from her lungs, the fragile girl gasped for breath. A bottomless pit emptied before her as she lay on a bridge of stone that spanned the great chasm. The events of the past several days had come full circle, as she found herself walking the dark stone platform, wondering what this place was. The small glowing orb she had seen before, levitated in the pillar of soft light upon the central pedestal. She approached it, not daring to touch it a second time.

"Who or …*what,* are you?" She asked, not knowing if this object could understand her. The bones in her body prickled as the implant translated into words, so that she could hear.

"*Who are you?*" It asked simply, it was a voice neither truly male nor female; but gentle, though it carried an undertone of immense power.

"I am Ala…" was all she could answer with a weak and humbled whisper. From below, the chasm erupted in a flood of voices, the same ones she had heard at the drilling site in the lower level of the central complex. They took the form of glowing wisps that weaved throughout the cavern, only to vanish like fading shadows. Millions of the iridescent streamers flocked in swirling clouds to shatter into nothingness. Once again, the voices slowly lulled into a hushed silence.

"*Your life invaded us, injured us; was killing us,*" the voice accused with disdain, "*Why did you leave your own essence, why do you seek to harm us?*" The voice demanded but the girl was confused by the question, referring to her 'essence', what the hell did that mean?

"I ...I don't understand," she admitted with humility. The droning whispers started once again, as if they were in debate over her response. The disembodied voice spoke again with a sense of renewed dignity towards the human girl.

"You are of Terra, you are of Earth," it stated firmly, *"We have spoken to your machines, your other-life; created from this form you embody called mankind. Your own recorded history proves that instead of existing in harmony on the world from which you came into being, your species chose to afflict it like a parasite. After you poisoned your own existence, the race of men left their homeworld to plague the stars. We have determined that your actions prove that you are a sickness, a disease,"* it charged upon her, *"We will purge you from us."*

Ala felt the overbearing weight of the entity's words, for it was all true, and here she was, alone to face the guilt of all mankind. Ala was stumped by the accusation, one to which she had no defense. Without question, it could certainly be perceived that humanity was an affliction upon the universe. Mankind had been quarantined on Earth for countless millennia, only to spread like a vile pestilence across the cosmos where we were not wanted nor belonged.

"You are right," the young woman began, knowing she was helpless against this alien phantom. It had wiped out an entire colony of thousands, commandeered every computerized AI on the planet and brought her here to face judgment. She figured she was dead either way, "The human race has a history of selfish violence and disregard for anyone or anything they don't understand," Ala retorted, knowing that the statement could logically refer to countless eons of strife as mankind has warred against itself over petty differences.

*"Understand this; your species is of Terra, of Earth. Mankind does not belong beyond the borders of its own essence, its own ...**mother**,"* the voice had given pause, as if searching to translate the proper term. *"Here, we are one, and I am all,"* the voice proceeded to interpret, illuminating Ala's perception, *"The world you call Earth is a living being, aware and conscious in a way your minds have yet to comprehend. You are one with her, yet your life has willfully injured and abandoned your essence in a cruel and calloused act of betrayal. Now your kind spreads to other worlds such as I, to commit these same atrocities."*

It took but a moment to sink in for Ala to realize; this wasn't some bodiless alien ghost she was speaking to, she was standing within it ...it was the planet! Renee had been right all along, the human species had a habit of not seeing anything that wasn't flesh and bone as intelligent life, we even considered animals as our lesser, and plant life was treated with a certain amount of disregard. We settled on distant worlds and raped their ecosystems for our own needs without a second thought to the harm that we caused; but this time we pissed off a whole planet, and it pissed right back in our faces. Ala looked at the small orb floating in the pillar of light and wondered, was there an entity like this somewhere in the depths of our own homeworld on Earth?

"You are Tranquility..." she pondered for a brief moment, "I think I understand now," Ala realized.

With a dizzy sigh, she felt as if she was going to faint. She had lived her whole life salvaging the losses of others, hunting for scraps to survive; and now she was thrown into a bigger picture of just how small and insignificant she truly was. Ala had grown up fighting for herself, never really caring about anyone else; there was too much risk in that. Her heart, her feelings, her own self-doubt; were all too fragile to open up to others. In her own selfish haste, she had chosen to leave BoB behind, a loyal friend who had risked everything to help her. She regretted having done that, and it weighed on her heavily.

"Tranquility ...that name will suffice, though we do not require one," the voice replied as the drumming of a thousand whispers echoed up from the chasm below.

"Then you should know that the robotic beings we left on the planet have changed and are trapped in a cycle of war; creating the very same problems, the same 'illness' that mankind itself, had become," Ala mentioned.

"We provided that form of life a sense of will and self-awareness to help serve us. Though now they no longer hear us, they no longer listen," the powerful words rang like the toll of a bell. Over the past few decades, the bots must have upgraded their own circuitry design several-fold from their original models; whatever quirk allowed this entity to communicate with the worker droids in the beginning, eventually became outdated.

Ala could now see that this world was a living being, and it considered the bots as a type of living creature. It actually wasn't a far stretch for the imagination, as robotics technicians had been working towards that end for centuries at playing God. However, true to our nature, we created them as slaves to serve our own needs instead of allowing them genuine unhindered sentience. This being, this *entity*, had given them a spark of its own life, forever changing them.

"If they should harm us, then they too will be purged

from existence," the voice gave a final note of their fate.

"Doing so would make you no better than the human race you so despise; it would be a cold act of betrayal against what ***you***, yourself, have given awareness," Ala charged back, "...and you would prove yourself to be just as cruel as the plague you call mankind."

As her harsh words rang back there was a rise and quell of the whispering voices from below, as if the entity was the voice of trillions of living things; their thoughts aligned as they considered the weight of her words.

"*As you are the Allah of your world, we will not destroy you*," it advised the young girl, who was oblivious to the mistaken connotation of her name for the title of some ancient deity, "*We will allow your continued existence as a prophet, and beg you to enlighten these metal beings to change their course*," it instructed, "*Note, however, we will not allow you to leave this world; and furthermore, if you should fail in this duty, we will destroy you all*."

"...As a prophet?" Ala whispered in marked confusion.

"*Yes, it is the title from your own historical records attained from the central machine that still speaks to us*," It announced, "*As for the metal ones, you will act as our medium, you will be our voice and our messenger.*"

Appointed with this unusual rank, a bright static charge suddenly danced across her cybernetic implant. Ala nearly jumped in alarm but the burst of electricity quickly dissipated. She would never forget the final words of the haunting presence that spoke to her.

"*The metal beings will listen to you now, as you are a part of them. Make them understand that they must not continue their current ways, and remember that their fate depends on you.*"

* * *

Location: Planet: Tranquility
              Avalon base station
Mission: Restoration Project
Log: 822T - closing entry

It has now been 54 cycles since I had risen from the dead and washed back upon that quiet shore deep below Outpost 9, emerging to find that the bots I had once feared no longer hunted me; somehow their aggression had been lulled by my altered implant, which had been touched by the entity. Since then, I have negotiated disputes between the rogue droids in the effort to bring an end to the violence between the warring factions. If you are reading this log, then you no doubt have reviewed the extensive records I have kept over the years. I had warned the hostile bots of the wrath and judgment they would face should they fail to heed my warnings. I was the appointed messenger after all; their living prophet, the voice of the spirits from the underworld.

It took great effort to rally the separate tribes of droids, for in their artificial eyes, I had created many miracles; educating them how to fabricate new components and resources from the data logs of the stations main computer banks. Truly, it was a time when the robots began to act with more humanity than mankind itself; their AI brains were self programming, and they have learned to care for the delicate homeworld they called Tranquility. In all these years, no ships have yet passed by this sector of the galaxy; apparently, the REVO Corporation had gone bankrupt since the failure of its flag colony.

Sadly, the Avalon project and the thousands of men and

women that had built it were all but forgotten. As you will find outlined in the records, I directed the bots to repair the hydroponic gardens and taught them how to care for the flora as they once had. It took decades to reverse the damage the colonists had done to the native soil, and over these years, I sent out mass armies of droids to replant the native vegetation. During the restoration project, entire landscapes were changed and new species of life now flourish. I should also note that the bots have evolved as well, their primary directives had been abolished and every combat model has been dismantled. Even now, the robots continued to alter and customize their own bodies toward their given labors; evidence of their sense of pride and individuality.

There came a day long past when I discovered that the murderous Hellbot model, known as the 'G' series, had actually stood for Renee's original 'Gaia' file, which she had hidden within the central computer. The robots had designed themselves after insects, which were recorded as the primary surviving species of our polluted Earth, and proved to be a vital part of the ecosystem.

This will be my last entry, as I am getting old and might not have much time left in this world. Settlers may yet stumble across this planet once again; and to those who might ignore the warnings from the orbiting beacon, you will find the small moon of Tranquility transformed into a virtual Eden. All I will ask is that you leave the bots to exist here in peace. I can only warn you not to land, for if you do, you will not be allowed to return from this sacred place. I've kept a dedicated record of my life here, in hopes that someone will know my story.

- End of file -

Avalon

During her reign, the once young and temperamental girl rose to control a vast legion of bots that obeyed her every command. Before a roaring fire, Ala, queen of the droids, sat upon her great steel throne; looking out over her vast court of robotic subjects and felt a wave of accomplishment wash through her old and tired body. She had fulfilled an empty chasm within herself and finally found true meaning and purpose to her life ...as strange and alien as it was.

Outside the vast castle walls of the central complex, the colorful and exotic gardens of this world now flourished. By the grace of the spirits of this land; once again, the underground streams rose to allow flowing rivers to nurture the surface. The bright valleys glistened with beauty from the fine mists of cool mountain springs to roaring waterfalls of deep indigo that flowed to the bright sandy shores of their tranquil seas.

Throughout the ages, this utopia remained hidden from the dying race of mankind that had spread itself so very thin across the galaxy. There were still those bold few pioneers that clung to such fragile hopes and dreams of finding a better world, who still look to the stars for their salvation. Those few who search hard enough might catch the twinkle of a long forgotten island, lost amongst the stars; where immortals still dwell in shining armor, a paradise of legend called Avalon.

*   *   *

About the Author

Michel Savage has been devoted to writing throughout his career. If one reads between the lines, they will find his novels revolve around the reminder that we are only borrowing our small place on this planet but for a brief period of time, and to take responsibility for the environment, for one another and all other living creatures with which we share this world. And in doing so, hopefully planting a seed in our conscience of the importance to preserve what is left of the wilds, our untainted woodlands, and ever-dwindling rain forests.

He has had the blessing of sharing his stories and artwork around the globe, which is a gift in itself, and would encourage others not to waste too much of their lives chasing someone else's dreams but to follow their own.

One of the most valuable lessons he has learned in his years is that there are far more important things in life than power and money, such as kindness, compassion, and consideration towards others.

...share that thought if you will.

Enter the Grey Forest
www.**GreyForest**.com

Also by
Michel Savage

Outlaws of Europa

The 2nd moon of Jupiter has been turned into a prison planet. Where for several generations, robot drone ships have been dumping the scum of the universe and are patrolled by a ring of advanced security satellites that would destroy any vessel attempting to land. After a century of research, old core samples from the ice reveal that the frozen oceans of Europa hold the base element of an immortality drug that can extend the human lifespan several-fold. Now greedy military corporations race for the new fountain of youth, only to discover they can't disable the orbiting sentry which was programmed to protect itself at all costs.

It appears the Confederation has a problem. How do they get past a self-evolving AI that has appointed itself as Warden, and furthermore, retake a planet roaming with Earth's worst criminals who might well be immortal themselves.

The Shadoworld Series
Shadow of the Sun

On a distant, slowly rotating world, Bronze Age tribes must migrate thought their lives to avoid the long cold death of nightfall. As of late, strange events have been deeply troubling their tribal elders; revealing evidence that something was lurking on the dark side.

As for a pair of young misfits, the ancient mystery is about to unfold; to reveal their peoples forgotten past, buried deep within the underworld, shrouded in the shadow of the sun.

Shadoworld - Veil of Shadows

Ash was an orphaned street urchin who grew up in the gutters of a desolate medieval city; his bitter youth spent picking pockets and snatching trinkets from the wealthy to survive.

Over the years his art for stealth and sharpened skills had drawn the attention of the Thieves Guild who took him into their folds. Little did they know that the boys tragic past would one day find itself woven within the treacherous schemes of a mysterious spider cult.

As of late, a series of chilling murders had befallen several nobles within the privileged upper districts. Their gruesome deaths had appeared to be centered around an ancient cursed skull, which had recently found its way into the hands of a rich collector. There were few who would trespass upon the strange realms of witchcraft and dark magic ...but a master thief does not fear those who dwell in darkness, for he is one with the shadows.

Shadoworld - Shadows Gate

Asra found himself alone in the middle of the barren sands, unable to remember who he was or how he had gotten there. Saved by a caravan of traveling gypsies, he entered into an exotic world of dancing acrobats, fortune tellers, and mystics who performed their skills for cheering crowds across the desert empires.

However, his destiny would change the day he stumbled upon a forbidden shrine to find a mythical creature entombed beneath its shattered ruins. Promises were whispered and a dark pact was made with the ancient demon; a bond of magic that would lead him on a perilous journey to reveal his forgotten past.

Michel Savage

Broken Mirror
Apophis 2029

Hurtling through space was an enormous tumbling rock known as MN4 our astronomers affectionately named after an ancient Egyptian god of destruction. Asteroid Apophis was the talk of the year that every scientific community on Earth was aware of, though its flyby in April 2029 was to be nothing more than a spectacular celestial event; but as warring nations were locked in global conflict, our civilization was unprepared for the devastation that followed in its wake.

Several years after governments fell and society dissolved a ragged pack of survivors stumble upon the buried truth, revealing what circumstances had led to the aftermath that ensued; leaving them to question their struggle to salvage what few splintered shards were left of our world that would forever define our bitter legacy.

Forgotten Future

At the edge of the world an impossible relic from the fables of antiquity has risen from the frozen wastelands of Antarctica. Professor Logan and his exploration team rush to investigate this historic find, but this unique discovery puts their lives in peril when they unearth the remnants of a long forgotten civilization left buried beneath the ice.

Within the twisting labyrinths below the melting glaciers they uncover an ancient culture which had perished from a mysterious cataclysm. They soon realize it was a polar shift which had caused their destruction, and our world was presently facing the same fate.

7 - The Fall

A strange and unexplained phenomenon led to the fall of civilization. It began on an evening like any other. The Sun had set on another day, but by the next morning, humanity realized that there were no more stars in the sky. Somehow, overnight, mankind had become alone in the universe and only an AI program knew why.

Witchwood
The Harvesting

Every day around the world hundreds of people go missing without a trace. Year after year, their numbers add up to millions of lost souls who are never to be seen again; and their numbers keep climbing ...this is where many of them went.

Project EVE

In the late 1940s after the 2nd World War, a classified government program was created in order to explore the military use of psychics to gain an advantage for their soldiers during armed conflict. At a remote laboratory in the mountains, a secret compound comprised of several hundred test subjects were trained to enhance their abilities with the goal of achieving the skills of telepathy and mind control.

Assigned to investigate this covert project, Walter Grant found himself entangled in a web of conspiracy and deceit when he discovered that the residents of the colony were being held captive by the scientists who had hidden the ugly truth behind their dangerous experiments.

At the heart of the project was a girl named Eve, whose extraordinary mind held the key, a child who would prove to them why humanity could not handle such power.

Michel Savage

The Faerylands Trilogy
I • The Grey Forest
II • Soulstorm Keep
III • Sorrowblade

Long, long ago the Faerie had roamed free, but for countless centuries now the fey themselves have remained unseen; hidden and withdrawn, shrouded within the boundaries of the Evermore. But just how they became imprisoned there was a mystery their own elders had forgotten or refused to speak of, and a subject of taboo among the ancients.

The Elvenborn had become a dying race, and now a strange and dreadful blight was encroaching upon their sanctuary. Ivy knew there was something terribly wrong with her world, something unspeakable her kind was hiding from. The Faerylands were vanishing, and she had to find out why.

Ivory
The Dreamkeepers

The Elvenborn were bestowed the task of healing their realm, a land left in chaos by the hands of men.

Limerick was but a simple bard who stumbled upon an epic quest, one that would test his courage and take him beyond the edges of the Faerylands. High in the mountains sat the ruins of Aldana, where the spirits of the forest gathered to bring balance to the world and end the dreadful blight of the Craven.

Along this journey, the young bard would learn that everything is not as it seems, and that dreams are but a shadow of something real.

Artwork from the Faerylands series available online

Enter the Grey Forest
www.**GreyForest**.com